倍斯特出版事業有限公司
Best Publishing Ltd.

Keywords and Phrases for
International Trade and Business

國貿人 英單句型
在全世界做生意
必備關鍵

看懂訂單了嗎？信用狀上寫了什麼？用英文怎麼催款？

掌握3大學習關鍵，和剛入行時的手忙腳亂Say bye!

劉美慧 (Amy) ◎ 著

看字彙導覽解說，不讓同事看你笑話！
輕鬆閱讀國貿高手趣味又專業的分享，字彙背景摸清了，即能在各流程上用「對」單字，解決不知如何用英文訂購、議價、出貨等窘境！

學字彙在E-mail怎麼寫、電話怎麼講，成為主管可信賴的萬能寫手、幫手！
熟悉各流程單字、句型的使用方式，在英文信件中正確「寫」出不可撤銷、可讓購等這些難字，和廠商／代理商用英文「談」交貨條件及付款條件！

用「聽」的記憶單字、句型，擺脫「不敢說」、「怕說錯」的困境！
聽外籍老師正統發音，確實記下單字念法，遇上客訴、出貨通關等緊急問題時，能從容回答！

Preface 作者序

　　這是我的第三本商用英文學習書，在第一本的作者序裡，我說到了「良心」這事兒（當然是吹噓我本人是個很有良心的人啊！哈！），而在第二本裡，我簡單說了一下我的青春情事，說了我在知識學習路上的幾個轉折點，請讀者用心做好當下的每一件事！那這一本的序言一定要來個更深沉、更有意義的議題啊～～好！就這麼辦！我們來好好說說「背單字」這件事！（什麼？這不是老掉牙的事嗎？這年頭不是強調不要背嗎？）好好好！為了不要引起反感，那我們改成來談……「記單字」！（還不是一樣？）哈！請好好聽我說，死「背」指的是一種手段、方法，而「記」可就是我們學習英文字彙的最終目標呢！要讓我們記得學到的英文字彙，方法的確很多，你可以不要死背硬背，但請你活學活用！在你每天工作中碰到的任何英文 E-mail 和文件，請用心用力看，裡頭的英文字一個都不要放過，多看幾次它的搭配詞與用法。而在學到了新的字，新的用法後，就請你想辦法現學現賣，寫 E-mail 也用、也給它說來用，找個時間也讓自己大聲唸出來，順道想個情境自己對話，造個句，甚至練習說篇小短文等等，為自己塑造一個英文學習的環境！

　　在商用英文的領域中，專業的詞彙與用法我們一定要會要懂，而要看懂或是能用英文說明各種相關的狀況，也還有很多有關的字彙該學，那……從何開始呢？你可以找幾本有用心、有良心、有認真寫的商用英文學習書來好好跟著學（請你猜猜看我要推薦你哪幾本呢？請見這篇序言的第一句……對，我相信你瞭了！呵呵！）。書有了，那要怎麼學呢？請你要求自己從頭讀到尾，每一個單元好好記個幾句，讓你自己熟到用膝蓋講都講得出來！這樣的紮實功夫一直持續做下去，不久後你一定會突然發現怎麼自己英文聽得懂了，變好了呢！最後，在此祈願各位親愛的讀者，在這條漫漫英文學習路上，能夠一路保持著活蹦亂跳、興味盎然的好奇心，且能學習著並快樂著，能夠獲得不斷精進的成就感！共勉之！

劉美慧 (Amy)

Editor 編者序

　　一切的專業都從基礎開始，在成為國貿高手之前，都要歷經許多磨鍊，其中國貿人常接觸的英文字彙（特別是專業術語）、句型，就是一個關卡，尤其對於非國貿科系的人來說更是如此，本書的企劃也因此誕生；它降低難度的門檻，以最簡明扼要的文字，介紹國貿必備流程，並一一帶入必備的單字、句型，進而套入口說、E-mail的基礎應用，非國貿科系的學習者都能馬上進入工作狀況，避免因為不懂國貿專業英文術語，而碰上的窘境，英文程度也能同步提升。

　　我們有信心，本書能兼顧「易學性」和「專業度」，絕對是引領讀者進入並熟悉國貿領域的入門寶典，100 % 實用！

編輯部敬上

Instructions 學習特色與使用說明

1 由內而外、循序漸進的國貿流程分類！碰上
不會的，可馬上查找，迅速解決問題！

Contents 目次

1 Part | 價格 Price

1-1 詢價 I'd like to **inquire** about...	014
1-2 報價 Our list price is...	020
1-3 折扣 We provide quantity **discounts**...	026
1-4 交貨條件 We offer under xxx shipping terms...	032
1-5 議價 Please support ... by offering your best price.	038
1-6 調價 We'll implement a price increase of x %.	044
1-7 計算報價 There will be a handling **fee**...	050
1-8 價格結構 The transfer price will be...	056
1-9 報價單 Attached is our quotation...	062

2 Part | 訂單 Place an order

2-1 下單 We'd like to **place** an **order** for...	068
2-2 改用網路下單 Please consider ordering online…	074
2-3 網路下單程序 **Browse** through the product catalogue...	080
2-4 訂貨確認 Please find attached your Order **Acknowledgment**...	086
2-5 修改訂單 We have to **adjust** the quantity of our order...	092
2-6 訂製訂單 If you'd like to request a custom order...	098

3 Part | 出貨 Shipment

3-1 出貨方式 You can choose from **express**, sea and air freight...	104
3-2 包裝 Please have it packed with...	110
3-3 出貨文件 Attached please find the complete set of shipping documents...	116
3-4 提單 Attached please find the AWB...	122
3-5 通關 The customs need clearance instructions from the recipient...	128

2 每單元皆有關鍵句型，重要字彙套色粗體，
馬上預覽每單元的重點句型和重要關鍵字！

3 每單元主題、關鍵例句一目了然！

4 國貿字彙藉由作者輕鬆的口吻，導覽解說該單元的情境與關鍵字彙，幫助讀者快速進入學習情境！

5 字彙導覽以列點的方式呈現，並將重要字彙套色，特以中英對照方式說明，專業知識與英文能力同步加分！搭上 MP3 邊聽邊學，還能做口譯練習！

1-1 詢價 Price Inquiry
I'd like to **inquire** about...

字彙 導覽解說　　Track 01

　　所有的交易幾乎都是從詢價或是詢問現貨狀況開始的，雖說萬事起頭難，但這樣的詢問難嗎？一點也不！但請注意一點，要問就要清清楚楚地問、問得清清楚楚，有了個好的基礎，後續就不會有一堆誤解出現喔！

1. **說產品**：要詢問產品，應一併列出型號（Catalog no.）、品名（Product name / Product description）、大小（Size）、規格（Specifications），以及網頁連結（Link）等資訊，將產品本體交待清楚！

2. **詢價格**：既然是詢價，當然一定要問產品的價格（Price），問有無折扣（Discount）好康，除此之外，也要好好瞭解一下與出貨相關的所有成本，像是預估的運費（Estimated freight）、手續費（Handling fee）與文件費（Documentation fee）等。

3. **詢供貨時間**：價格之外的一大詢問要點就是（Availability status）了，也要問問從接單到出貨的準備時間（Lead time）有多長！

字彙 應用搶先看：E-mail 會這麼寫！

1. I'd like to inquire about your PA0925 Extendable Selfie Stick which I've seen its information on your website. I'm highly interested in learning more about it. Please let me know its price and availability status.
   我想要詢問貴公司的 PA0925 伸縮自拍神器，我在您們的網站上有看到了這項產品的資訊，我很有興趣，想要多瞭解一些，還請您告訴我它的價格與現貨狀況。

2. We're interested in your CPY1202 product and would like to know its price, availability status and also the estimated freight cost to Taiwan. Please inform. If there are any additional fees, e.g. handling fee, please tell us as well. Thanks.
   我們對您的 CPY1202 產品有興趣，想知道它的價格與現貨狀況，以及貨到臺灣的預估運費，還請告知。若還有像是手續費這類額外收取的費用，也請一併告知，謝謝。

Part 1 價格

6 貼心的書側索引，呼應學習內容，方便查找，也加深學習印象！

7 字彙應用搶先看，先看關鍵字於 E-mail 中的應用！關鍵字套色、重點句型標上底線，馬上抓到重點！

8 這裡有 MP3 可以聽！不要錯過了！

9 重點字彙中英部分皆有套色，不怕迷失而突然找不到重點，提升學習效率！

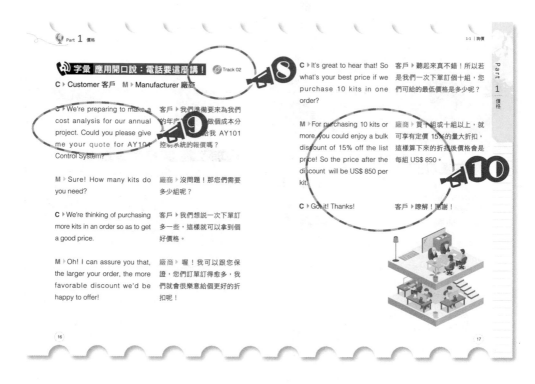

字彙 應用開口說：電話要這麼講！　　Track 02

C ▶ Customer 客戶　　M ▶ Manufacturer 廠商

C ▶ We're preparing to make a cost analysis for our annual project. Could you please give me your quote for AY101 Control System?

客戶 ▶ 我們準備要來為我們的年度專案做個成本分析，能不能給我 AY101 控制系統的報價嗎？

M ▶ Sure! How many kits do you need?

廠商 ▶ 沒問題！那您們需要多少組呢？

C ▶ We're thinking of purchasing more kits in an order so as to get a good price.

客戶 ▶ 我們想說一次下單訂多一些，這樣就可以拿到個好價格。

M ▶ Oh! I can assure you that, the larger your order, the more favorable discount we'd be happy to offer!

廠商 ▶ 喔！我可以跟您保證，您們訂單訂得愈多，我們就會很樂意給個更好的折扣呢！

C ▶ It's great to hear that! So what's your best price if we purchase 10 kits in one order?

客戶 ▶ 聽起來真不錯！所以若是我們一次下單訂個十組，您們可給的最低價格是多少呢？

M ▶ For purchasing 10 kits or more, you could enjoy a bulk discount of 15% off the list price! So the price after the discount will be US$ 850 per kit.

廠商 ▶ 買十組或十組以上，就可享有定價 15% 的量大折扣，這樣算下來的折扣後價格會是每組 US$ 850。

C ▶ Got it! Thanks!

客戶 ▶ 瞭解！謝謝！

10 對話中英文對照，輕鬆閱讀、好學！

11

精華收錄該國貿流程最重要的單字與例句，透徹了解該字彙的用法。例句更和國貿業務密切連結，加深學習印象！

字字 對較說分明

Track 03

availability [ə͵velə`bɪlətɪ] *n.* 現貨狀況、可得到的物（人）

例 The vendor's website allows us to check the price and also availability status of all their products.
這家供應商的網站可讓我們查詢他們所有產品的價格和現貨狀況。

catalog [`kætəlɔg] *n.* 型錄、目錄 = catalogue（英式拼法）

例 Please confirm the catalog number and provide the description of the item you are looking for.
請確認你所要找的產品的型號，也請告知其品名為何。

estimate [`ɛstə͵met] *v.* *n.* 估計

例 An estimated quote for the quantity requested, 5kg, would be US$ 1,800.00.
對於你所要求的 5kg 這個量，我們所估算的報價會是 US$ 1,800.00。

相關字 conservative estimate 保守的估計；rough estimate 粗略的估計

inquire [ɪn`kwaɪr] *v.* 詢問

例 Ann inquired about Summit Company's newly launched control system for making comparison with other similar products.
安詢問了高峰公司新推出的控制系統，藉以跟相似的產品來做個比較。

相關字 inquiry [ɪn`kwaɪrɪ] *n.* 詢問

lead time [lid taɪm] 訂單準備時間、出貨準備期

例 If your customer wants 10 kits from one single lot, the lead time would be 2-3 weeks from receipt of order. 如果你的客戶要求 10 組都來自於同一個批次，那麼出貨準備期就會是接單後的 2～3 個星期。

quote [kwot] *n.* 報價、報價單

例 Please let me know what quantity the customer will need so that I can develop an official quote for you. 請告訴我客戶需要的量有多少，這樣我就可以給你個正式的報價。

其他字義 *v.* 報價、引用

相關字 quotation [kwo`tefən] *n.* 報價、報價單

12

還有相關字彙整理，一次學會字彙不同詞性的變化與相關字詞搭配，快速累積字彙量！專業力倍增！

Contents 目次

1 Part | 價格 Price

1-1 詢價 I'd like to **inquire** about... 014

1-2 報價 Our list price is... 020

1-3 折扣 We provide quantity **discounts**... 026

1-4 交貨條件 We offer under xxx shipping terms... 032

1-5 議價 Please support ... by offering your best price. 038

1-6 調價 We'll implement a price increase of x %. 044

1-7 計算報價 There will be a handling **fee**... 050

1-8 價格結構 The transfer price will be... 056

1-9 報價單 Attached is our quotation... 062

2 Part | 訂單 Order

2-1 下單 We'd like to **place** an **order** for··· 068

2-2 改用網路下單 Please consider ordering online⋯ 074

2-3 網路下單程序 **Browse** through the product

catalogue... 080

2-4 訂貨確認 Please find attached your Order

Acknowledgment. 086

2-5 修改訂單 We have to **adjust** the quantity of our

order... 092

2-6 訂製訂單 If you'd like to request a **custom** order... 098

3 Part | 出貨 Shipment

3-1 出貨方式 You can choose from

express, sea and air freight... 104

3-2 包裝 Please have it packed with... 110

3-3 出貨文件 Attached please find the complete set of

shipping documents... 116

3-4 提單 Attached please find the AWB... 122

3-5 通關 The customs need clearance instructions from the

recipient... 128

4 Part | 付款 Payment

4-1 付款條件 If you are sending the payment using... 134

4-2 付款方式 We accept ... as payment methods. 140

4-3 信用狀 We can accept Letter of Credit at sight... 146

4-4 催款 Our records indicate the attached invoice is past **due**. 152

4-5 對帳單 I have attached a **statement** of your account. 158

5 Part | 客服與客訴 Customer service and complaints

5-1 索取產品資料 I've attached the **manual** for your review. 164

5-2 索取樣品 Free samples are available upon request... 170

5-3 索取官方證明文件 An export **license** must be obtained... 176

5-4 到貨問題 If you find that your goods are **faulty** on arrival... 182

5-5 保固服務 We shall repair the defective product covered by the **warranty**. 188

5-6 退貨政策 Products may be returned with our **permission**... 194

5-7 辦理退貨 All **returns** must be **authorized** by an RMA Number. 200

5-8 退款 We recommend returning for a **refund**... 206

5-9 罰款 There will be a x % **penalty** per day for delivery delay. 212

6 Part | 業務與行銷 Sales and marketing

6-1 業務會議 Please see the tentative **agenda** for our conference... 218

6-2 安排會議 We'd like to schedule a conference call to discuss... 224

6-3 業績檢討 The revenue has risen by x %... 230

6-4 展覽 If you plan on attending the Annual Meeting... 236

6-5 參展準備 We'll provide catalogs for you to distribute at... 242

6-6 促銷活動 We're offering a **promotion** to our distributors... 248

7 Part | 教育訓練 Training

7-1 訓練課程 We recommend you join us for the sales training... 254

7-2 線上研討會 Our product training **webinar** will be hosted on... 260

7-3 實體研討會 We will **organize** a seminar in the conference... 266

8 Part | 合作／代理關係 Cooperation and agency relationship

8-1 公司簡介 Our company was **established** in yyyy... 272

8-2 獨家代理 We authorize XXX as the exclusive

distributor... 278

8-3 非獨家代理 Our policy is not to give exclusivity... 284

8-4 購併 XXX was acquired by XXX. 290

8-5 人事異動 I just wanted to inform you that I'll soon be

leaving... 296

1-1 詢價 Price Inquiry

I'd like to **inquire** about...

字彙 導覽解說

　　所有的交易幾乎都是從詢價或是詢問現貨狀況開始的，雖説萬事起頭難，但這樣的詢問難嗎？一點也不！但請注意一點，要問就要清清楚楚地問、問得清清楚楚，有了個好的基礎，後頭才不會有一堆誤解出現喔！

1. **說產品**：要詢問產品，應一併列出型號（Catalog no.）、品名（Product name / Product description）、大小（Size）、規格（Specifications），以及網頁連結（Link）等資訊，將產品本體交待清楚！

2. **詢價格**：既然是詢價，當然一定要問問產品的價格（Price），問有無折扣（Discount）好康，除此之外，也要好好瞭解一下與出貨相關的所有成本，像是預估的運費（Estimated freight）、手續費（Handling fee）或文件費（Documentation fee）等。

3. **詢供貨時間**：價格之外的一大詢問要點就是現貨狀況
（Availability status）了，也要問問從接單到出貨的出貨準
備時間（Lead time）有多長！

✉ 字彙 應用搶先看：E-mail 會這麼寫！

1. I'd like to inquire about your PA0925 Extendable Selfie
Stick which I've seen its information on your website. I'm
highly interested in learning more about it. Please let me
know its price and availability status.
我想要詢問貴公司的 PA0925 伸縮自拍神器，我在您們的網
站上有看到了這項產品的資訊，我很有興趣，想要多瞭解一
些，還請您告訴我它的價格與現貨狀況。

2. We're interested in your CPY1202 product and would like
to know its price, availability status and also the estimated
freight cost to Taiwan. Please inform. If there are any
additional fees, e.g. handling fee, please tell us as well.
Thanks.
我們對您的 CPY1202 產品有興趣，想知道它的價格與現貨狀
況，以及貨到臺灣的預估運費，還請告知。若還有像是手續
費這類得額外收取的費用，也請一併告知，謝謝。

 **字彙** 應用開口說：電話要這麼講！ Track 02

C ▶ Customer 客戶 **M** ▶ Manufacturer 廠商

C ▶ We're preparing to make a cost analysis for our annual project. Could you please give me your quote for AY101 Control System?

客戶 ▶ 我們準備要來為我們的年度採購計畫做個成本分析，請問您能給我 AY101 控制系統的報價嗎？

M ▶ Sure! How many kits do you need?

廠商 ▶ 沒問題！那您們需要多少組呢？

C ▶ We're thinking of purchasing more kits in an order so as to get a good price.

客戶 ▶ 我們想說一次下單訂多一些，這樣就可以拿到個好價格。

M ▶ Oh! I can assure you that, the larger your order, the more favorable discount we'd be happy to offer!

廠商 ▶ 喔！我可以跟您保證，您們訂單訂得愈多，我們就會很樂意給個更好的折扣呢！

C ▶ It's great to hear that! So what's your best price if we purchase 10 kits in one order?

客戶 ▶ 聽起來真不錯！所以若是我們一次下單訂個十組，您們可給的最低價格是多少呢？

M ▶ For purchasing 10 kits or more, you could enjoy a bulk discount of 15% off the list price! So the price after the discount will be US$ 850 per kit.

廠商 ▶ 買十組或十組以上，就可享有定價 15%的量大折扣，這樣算下來的折扣後價格會是每組 US$ 850。

C ▶ Got it! Thanks!

客戶 ▶ 瞭解！謝謝！

字字 計較說分明

availability [əˌveləˈbɪlətɪ] *n.* 現貨狀況、可得到的物（人）

例 The vendor's website allows us to check the price and also availability status of all their products.

這家供應商的網站可讓我們查詢他們所有產品的價格和現貨狀況。

---

catalog [ˈkætələɡ] *n.* 型錄、目錄 = catalogue（英式拼法）

例 Please confirm the catalog number and provide the description of the item you are looking for.

請確認你所要找的產品的型號，也請告知其品名為何。

---

estimate [ˈɛstəˌmet] *v.* *n.* 估計

例 An estimated quote for the quantity requested, 5kg, would be US$ 1,800.00.

對於你所要求的 5kg 這個量，我們所估算的報價會是 US$ 1,800.00。

搭配詞 conservative estimate 保守的估計；rough estimate 粗略的估計

inquire [ɪnˋkwaɪr]　*v.*　詢問

例 Ann inquired about Summit Company's newly launched control system for making comparison with other similar products.

安詢問了高峰公司新推出的控制器，以跟其他相似的產品來做個比較。

相關字 inquiry *[ɪnˋkwaɪrɪ]*　*n.*　詢問

---

lead time [lid taɪm] 訂單準備時間、出貨準備期

例 If your customer wants 10 kits from one single lot, the lead time would be 2-3 weeks from receipt of order. 如果你的客戶要求 10 組都來自於同一個批次，那麼出貨準備期就會是接單後的 2～3 個星期。

---

quote [kwot]　*n.*　報價、報價單

例 Please let me know what quantity the customer will need so that I can develop an official quote for you. 請告訴我客戶需要的量有多少，這樣我就可以給你個正式的報價。

其他字義　*v.*　報價、引用

相關字 quotation *[kwoˋteʃən]*　*n.*　報價、報價單

1-2 報價 Quote

Our list price is...

字彙 導覽解說

　　廠商報價雖說就是報個價格，但也常有客戶拿到報價後得要左猜右想，並不是數字看不懂，而是看不透跟價格配套的相關條件。所以，我們這就來看看報價這事錢裡錢外的細節囉！

1. **價格種類**：廠商列在網站和型錄上的價格都是定價（List price），若詢價方是代理商，則廠商會報代理商價格（Distributor price），或稱移轉價格（Transfer price），加計代理商的適用折扣（Applied discount）。若是直接報價給使用者的價格，則稱為最終使用者價格（End user price）。

2. **金額**：要解讀報價金額，得注意廠商報價的幣別（Currency），看看所報的是單價（Unit price）、整組價格（Kit price），或是有最小訂單要求（Minimum order requirement）的規定。

3. **報價效期**：廠商回覆報價時，有時會加註報價的到期日

（Expiration date），或是告知此價格有效（valid）的期間
與條件。

✉ 字彙 應用搶先看：E-mail 會這麼寫！

1. <u>Our list price for S-1000 Calcium Tablets is US$ 100 and
   you could receive our 40% distributor discount for a price
   of US$ 60 per box.</u> Attached please find our official quote
   for 500 boxes. Please note that the quote is valid through
   December 31, 2016.
   <u>我們 S-1000 鈣片的定價為 US$ 100，您可享有 40%的代理
   商折扣，每盒的折扣後價格為 US$ 60。</u>在此附上我們 500
   盒的正式報價單，請注意此報價至 2016 年 12 月 31 日前有
   效。

2. The quote attached reflects the transfer price which your
   typical distributor discount is applied. Please be sure to
   reference the quote # at the time of order placement in
   order to guarantee the correct pricing.
   附上的報價單所列的是移轉價格，有加計了給您們的一般代
   理商折扣。下單時請務必加註報價單單號，以確保我們能給
   您正確的價格。

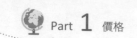
字彙 應用開口說：電話要這麼講！　Track 05

D ▶ Distributor 代理商　　**M** ▶ Manufacturer 廠商

D ▶ We're interested in your AC-500 enzyme kit. Could you tell us its price?

代理商 ▶ 我們對 AC-500 酵素組有興趣，您能告訴我它的價格嗎？

M ▶ Sure! The unit price is US$ 100.

廠商 ▶ 當然可以！它的單價是 US$ 100。

D ▶ Is US$ 100 our distributor price?

代理商 ▶ US$ 100 這個價格是給我們的代理商價格嗎？

M ▶ Oh! It's the list price. You can still get 30% standard distributor discount.

廠商 ▶ 喔！這是定價，您一樣可以拿到標準的 30% 代理商折扣。

D ▶ I see. So could we order only 1 kit or do you need us to order more like our last case?

代理商 ▶ 瞭解，所以我們可以只訂 1 組，還是也要跟我們上一個案子一樣得訂個好幾組呢？

M ▶ Wow, you did remind me of this important requirement! Yes! You have to order 5 at least because we've stipulated a minimum order quantity of this item as well.

廠商 ▶ 哇！您倒真提醒了我這個重要的規定呢！是的，您至少得買 5 組，因為我們對這一項產品也有制定了個最小訂購量的規定。

D ▶ Okay! Would you please e-mail me your official quote for... 5 kits?

代理商 ▶ 好的，那麼請您 e-mail 給我⋯⋯5 組的正式報價單，好嗎？

M ▶ Not a problem. I'll do whatever you say!

廠商 ▶ 沒問題！您說的我都會照辦！

字字 計較說分明

 Track 06

apply [ə`plaɪ]   *v.*   應用、使適用

例 If you purchase only 3 kits, there will be no special price and your usual distributor discount would apply.

若是您只買 3 組，就不會有特價，而是適用您平常所享的代理商折扣。

相關字 application [ˏæplə`keʃən]   *n.*   申請、用途、應用軟體（也就是大家說得熟透的「APP」！）

applicant [`æpləkənt]   *n.*   申請人

applicable [`æplɪkəbḷ]   *adj.*   適宜的

---

currency [`kɝ-ənsɪ]   *n.*   貨幣

例 Please specify the currency (USD, EUR or GBP) which you will be using to pay for this transaction.

請您指明會用哪一種貨幣（美金、歐元或英鎊）來支付這筆交易的貨款。

相關字 current [`kɝ-ənt]   *adj.*   現今的、通用的

---

expiration [ˏɛkspə`reʃən]   *n.*   期滿 = expiry [ɪk`spaɪrɪ]

例 I will be happy to give you the expiration information of available lots when you are closer to placing the order.

我很樂意在您快要下單前，提供現有批次到期日的資訊給您。

相關字 expire *[ɪkˋspaɪr]* v. 滿期

例 This quotation will expire in one month.

此報價一個月內有效。

---

transfer [ˋtrænsfɚ] *n.* 轉讓、轉帳 [trænsˋfɚ] *v.*

例 The product's distributor price is EUR 1.500,00 per 1 kg. There will also be an extra EUR 30,00 fee to cover bank charges incurred from international wire transfer.

這項產品每 1kg 的代理商單價為 1,500 歐元，另外，對於國際匯款，我們還會加收 30 歐元的國際匯款轉帳的銀行手續費。

---

valid [ˋvælɪd] *adj.* 有效的

例 This pricing is only valid on the single order of 10 kits or more.

一次下單 10 組或更多量時，才能適用此價格。

1-3 折扣 Discount

We provide quantity **discounts...**

字彙 導覽解說

1. **折扣種類**：折扣是吸引買方注意、促成訂單的利器，而説起折扣，除了前面單元所説到的代理商折扣（Distributor discount）之外，廠商最常運用的就是數量折扣（Quantity / Volume discount）了，若要吸引買方在付款上阿莎力，馬上付清全額，則會給出現金折扣（Cash Discount）或是提前付款折扣（Settlement Discount）的優惠條件。

2. **折扣設計**：在説明折扣方案（Discount program）或折扣結構（Discount structure）時，會説到適用的產品、數量與折扣率（Discount rate），而在折扣率的設計上，有的也會分出一般 / 固定 / 標準折扣（General / Regular / Standard discount）與額外的折扣（Additional discount、Extra discount）。

✉ 字彙 應用搶先看：E-mail 會這麼寫！

1. We recently instituted a volume discount program as attached to make it easier for you to get even greater discount values on your purchases.

   我們最近訂定了數量折扣方案如附，讓您採購時更容易享受到更大的折扣。

2. <u>We do provide</u> quantity discounts <u>on our products.</u> We encourage you to make your purchases in these larger quantities to enjoy the discount.

   <u>我們對產品有提供數量折扣</u>，建議您在數量上多採購一些，以享有折扣的優惠。

3. By ordering 2 or more vials of the same product and pack size, you will benefit from our new discount program. You can save up to 25%.

   若對同產品、同包裝訂購的量達兩瓶或兩瓶以上時，就可適用我們新的折扣方案，可以替您節省高達 25%的成本。

字彙 應用開口說：電話要這麼講！ Track 08

D ▶ Distributor 代理商 M ▶ Manufacturer 廠商

D ▶ Our customer would like to try your FM1 system. Could you give him a special discount for his first trial order?

代理商▶ 有個客戶想要試用您們的 FM1 系統，請問您對他這份首次試用訂單能給個特別折扣嗎？

M ▶ For only 1 kit, sorry but we are not able to offer any additional discount. Your regular discount would apply in this case.

廠商 ▶ 只有一組的話，很抱歉我們沒得提供任何的額外折扣，可給的就是您的固定折扣了。

D ▶ Please re-consider because this customer plays a key role in the industry and their demand will be high in the future.

代理商▶ 請再考慮一下，因為這個客戶在這個產業裡有著舉足輕重的地位，而且他們將來的需求量也會很大。

M ▶ Hmm... Considering the potential of the customer, I think I can offer you a 5% additional discount, but it's just for this one time!

廠商 ▶ 嗯……，想想這個客戶的潛力，我們倒是可以給個 5%的額外折扣，不過就只有這次喔！

D ▶ Thanks for your support!

代理商 ▶ 謝謝您的支持！

M ▶ We'll look forward to the customer's initial order and also the following bulk order!

廠商 ▶ 那我們就期待您發來客戶這次首次下單的訂單，也期待他們之後的大單囉！

D ▶ Yeah! Please wait for our good news!

代理商 ▶ 好啊！請等著我們的好消息囉！

字字 計較說分明

Track 09

benefit [`bɛnəfɪt] v. 受惠

例 Please be reminded to order by this Friday so as to benefit from the reduced fees.

提醒您在星期五前下單，以享受費用減價優惠。

其他字義 n. 好處；津貼；福利

相關字 mutual benefit 互惠互利、共同利益

搭配詞 beneficial [,bɛnə`fɪʃəl] adj. 有益的

beneficiary [,bɛnə`fɪʃərɪ] n. 受益人

---

discount [`dɪskaʊnt] n. v. 折扣

例 Since we are giving these products a high discount, we expect you to lower your margin in order to provide a competitive offer to the customer.

既然對這些產品我們給了您們很大的折扣，我們也希望您們能調降利潤，報個有競爭力的價格給客戶。

---

general [`dʒɛnərəl] adj. 一般的

例 Attached is a general quote for our smallest standard pack size.

附上我們對最小標準包裝產品的一般報價。

搭配詞 in general 一般地；generally speaking 一般來說；general terms and conditions 一般條款

regular [ˋrɛgjələ]　*adj.*　固定的、正常的

例 This product can be purchased from our regular inventory for $250.00.

這項產品可從我們的固定存貨來供貨，價格為$250.00。

volume [ˋvɑljəm]　*n.*　（生產、交易等）量、額

例 Orders placed on Jan. 4th will not be able to be shipped out that same day due to the large volume of orders we will have after the holidays.

1/4 所下的訂單將無法在當天出貨, 因我們在假期後所要消化的訂單量很大。

其他字義 體積、容積、卷、冊

1-4 交貨條件 Shipping Terms

We offer under xxx shipping terms...

字彙 導覽解說

 Track 10

交貨條件是國貿知識裡的大要點，分類很多，説法與細節也不少，就讓我們來把所有交貨條件一起「表」起來看囉！

頭字語	英文全稱	中文
EXW	Ex-Works	工廠交貨價
FOB	Free On Board	船上交貨價
FCA	Free Carrier	運送人交貨價
CFR/ CNF	Cost and Freight	運費內含價
CIF	Cost, Insurance and Freight	運保費內含價
DAP	Delivered at Place	目的地交貨價
FAS	Free Alongside Ship	船邊交貨價
DAT	Delivered at Terminal	終點站交貨價
CPT	Carriage Paid to	運費付訖交貨價

CIP	Carriage and Insurance Paid to	運保費付訖交貨價
DDP	Delivered Duties Paid	稅訖交貨價

✉ 字彙 應用搶先看：E-mail 會這麼寫！

1. The price for KT-0710 is $1185.00 per kit FOB Seattle. Freight and handling costs are additional and depend on the quantity ordered.

   每組 KT-0710 的西雅圖交貨 FOB 價格為$1185.00，運費與處理費皆須另計，金額視訂購數量而定。

2. Your distributor price is EUR 250,00 per kit, ex works Frankfurt, excluding shipping and handling costs, etc.

   給您的代理商價格為每組 250 歐元，此為法蘭克福工廠交貨價，不含運費及處理手續費等費用。

3. We're pleased to offer you the following quotation, under CIF shipping terms. We'll pay for both freight charges and insurance.

   我們很樂意給您報價如下，交貨條件為 CIF，我們將會負擔運費及保險費。

 Track 11

字彙 應用開口說：電話要這麼講！

B ▶ Buyer 買方   S ▶ Seller 賣方

B ▶ We're currently evaluating the purchase of your AL-01 Instrument. Could you please tell me its price?

買方 ▶ 我們正在評估個採購案，想購買您們的 AL-01 儀器，能不能請您告訴我它的價格呢？

S ▶ Sure! The list price is US$ 1,500 per set.

賣方 ▶ 當然可以！每套儀器的定價是 US$ 1,500。

B ▶ Is this your FOB price?

買方 ▶ 這是您們的 FOB 價格嗎？

S ▶ Yes, we always offer FOB quotes which include all related costs to get the goods to our airport.

賣方 ▶ 是的，我們都是報 FOB 價格，貨品到我們機場前的所有相關成本都會包含在裡頭。

B ▶ Please also let me know your CIF price. We prefer that its insurance as well as freight

買方 ▶ 也請告訴我您們的 CIF 價格，我們想要保險費和運費也加計在您們的價格

are to be covered by your side. By the way, we're located in Taiwan.

裡。對了，我們的所在地是在台灣。

S ▶ I see. I'll check the insurance rate and the freight charge from San Diego to your destination and then quote you our CIF price.

賣方 ▶ 瞭解，我會去問問保險費率，也會查一下從聖地牙哥到您們目的地的運費，再報給您我們的 CIF 價格。

B ▶ Thanks! I look forward to it!

買方 ▶ 謝謝了！那我就等您答覆囉！

字字 計較說分明

 Track 12

carrier [`kærɪɚ] *n.* 運送人、運輸業者

例 The international freight costs of the previous carrier are very high when shipping to a few locations. We will search for an international carrier that is more affordable.

先前運輸公司出到幾個地點的國際運費很高，我們會找找其他收費比較划算的國際運輸公司。

搭配詞 freight carrier 貨運公司

---

destination [ˌdɛstə`neʃən] *n.* 目的地

例 We need a certification stating that the product is to be applied exclusively for research use within the country of destination.

我們需要一份證明，說明這項產品將僅供目的地國家境內研究用。

---

exclude [ɪk`sklud] *v.* 不包括、排除

例 This product is available and the price is $595 USD per kit excluding shipping charges.

這項產品有現貨，單價為美金$595，不包含運費。

反義詞 include *[ɪn`klud] v.* 包括

相關字 exclusive *[ɪk`sklusɪv] adj.* 除外的、獨家的

exclusive of（不包括）＋ n.

exclusivity *[ˌɪksklu ˈsɪvɪtɪ]*　*n.*　獨家、獨有

搭配詞 exclusive distributor 獨家代理商

---

freight [fret]　*n.*　運費、貨運、（運輸的）貨物

例 Please give us the package's gross weight and dimension for us to check the freight with our courier agent.

請告訴我們出貨包裝的毛重與尺寸，我們要跟這裡快遞公司報的運費比較一下。

搭配詞 air / sea freight 空 / 海運

freight prepaid / collect 運費預付 / 到付

---

insurance [ɪnˋʃʊrəns]　*n.*　保險費

例 The total cost of a landed shipment includes purchase price, freight, insurance, and other costs up to the port of destination.

貨運的落地成本總額包含了產品買價、運費、保險，以及抵達目的地機場／港口前的所有其他成本。

1-5 議價 Price Negotiation

Please support... by offering your best price.

字彙 導覽解說

1. **限制何在**：若是代理商要跟廠商議價，則會說到客戶端在預算（budget）上的限制（limitation），也會從市場的競爭（competition）態勢來好好分析一下，說明一下為何廠商原先的報價難做。

2. **美好前景**：說完了限制，就該來些正面的誘因了！要說服廠商給個好價格，當然要來強調一下客戶的潛力（potential）及在市場上的影響力（influence），再來，還可從客戶幾年來不離不棄的忠誠度（loyalty）來好好地對廠商動之以情！

3. **談判時刻來了**：當代理商說完情與理之後，就要開始角力了！在談判、協商（negotiation）的過程中，看看廠商肯不肯支持（support）、能不能順應（accommodate）要求，妥協與讓步（compromise、meet halfway），讓談判能夠順利結束，共同締造雙贏的局面（win-win situation）！

✉ 字彙 應用搶先看：E-mail 會這麼寫！

1. Unfortunately, your offer is high while our customer's budget is limited. For your information, the customer has a lot of potential of placing bulk orders in the future, and also has the power to influence quite a few users in the market.

   但您報來的價格高，而我們客戶的預算卻很有限。也讓您知道一下，這個客戶未來很有潛力下大筆的訂單，也有能力影響市場上的其他使用者。

2. To compete with our arch-rival and let this key customer switch to buy from us, we hope you could support this project by offering your best bottom line price. We'll also lower our margin to get the most competitive price to the customer.

   為了跟我們的主要競爭對手競爭，並為了讓這個重要客戶轉而成為我們的主顧，我們希望您可以提供支援，報給我們您的最底價，而我們也會降低我們的利潤，讓報給客戶的價格能夠最具競爭力。

字彙 應用開口說：電話要這麼講！   Track 14

D ▸ Distributor 代理商   **M ▸** Manufacturer 廠商

D ▸ You know TopTech adopted a low price strategy since last year, right? Now they even knocked down their price to a new low of US$ 2,000!

代理商 ▸ 你知道尖端科技從去年就採取低價策略，對吧？現在他們居然下殺到 US$ 2,000 這個創新低的價格耶！

M ▸ No way!

廠商 ▸ 不可能！

D ▸ It's true! So it's really hard for us to compete with them. We need your help to increase the discount rate to 50%.

代理商 ▸ 真的！所以要跟他們競爭真的有難，我們需要你的協助，看能否把折扣率調高到 50％。

M ▸ We're willing to support you but unfortunately, we're unable to accommodate your request of such a large discount!

廠商 ▸ 我們願意協助你們，但對於這麼高折扣率的要求，抱歉我們真的無法配合耶！

D ▶ What's the largest discount you could offer to us?

代理商 ▶ 那你能給的最大折扣會是多少呢？

M ▶ I can approve 40% off. That's the best I can do! I suggest you decrease your margin as well to bring the offer to the customer more competitive.

廠商 ▶ 我最多可給到 40%！建議你們也把利潤率調降，好能給客戶一個更有競爭力的價格。

D ▶ We'll do that and we'll also do whatever it takes to win over the competition!

代理商 ▶ 我們會的，而且我們也會盡所有可能的努力來贏得這場競爭！

 字字 計較說分明

budget [`bʌdʒɪt]   *n.*   預算

例 Our budget is extremely limited. Please support this project by offering a special discount to us.

因為我們的預算極為有限，請您給予支援，提供特別折扣給我們。

搭配詞 a tight budget 預算緊、over budget 超出預算

---

competition [ˌkɑmpə`tɪʃən]   *n.*   競爭

例 With more manufacturers vying for the market share, we'll unavoidably face intense competition.

面對愈來愈多的廠商爭奪各自的市場佔有率，我們免不了將會面臨激烈的競爭。

搭配詞 cut-throat / fierce / stiff / keen / intense / tough competition 激烈的競爭

---

compromise [`kɑmprə͵maɪz]   *n.*   *v.*   妥協、和解、妥協方案、危及

例 I am happy that we are able to reach a compromise. We will accept your proposal for payment as described in your last e-mail.

我很高興我們雙方能夠達成妥協，我們會接受您前一封

e-mail 所提出的付款方式。

其他字義 　*v.* 　讓步；危及、損害；妥協。

---

influence [`ɪnfluəns] 　*n.* 　*v.* 　影響

例 The research institute has a substantial influence on the development of this industry.

這間研究機構對此產業的發展有很大的影響力。

---

negotiate [nɪ`goʃɪˌet] 　*v.* 　協商、談判

例 If the customer will be purchasing all 20 kits in one order, there may be room for negotiating a bigger discount.

若是客戶會一次下單訂購 20 組，那就能有更大折扣的協商空間。

---

potential [pə`tɛnʃəl] 　*n.* 　潛力、可能性；*adj.* 　潛在的、可能的

例 We'd like to understand in more detail the potential of this product in your market.

對於這項產品在你們市場上的潛力，我們想要有更多的瞭解。

1-6 調價 Price Adjustment

We'll implement a price increase of x %.

字彙 導覽解說　　　Track 16

1. **要調價囉**：價格調整（adjustment）有九成五都是往上調（price increase、price rise、price augmentation、raising the prices、marking up the prices），極為難得才會遇到原廠有調降（price cut、price reduction、a drop / fall in prices）的非常作法！

2. **非調不可的原因**：有些原廠的價格調整是每年一次（on an annual basis），有些廠商調漲價格是因為成本增加（rising costs），而所提及的成本會包括有生產（production）、原料（raw material）、包裝（packaging）、人力（labor）、運輸（transportation）等成本。

3. **啟用新價格**：調價一出，一定會說個明白，告知何時新價會生效（go / come / put into effect、take effect），會定出生效日（effective date），明確告知目前舊價（current / old

prices）何日正式退位！

字彙 應用搶先看：E-mail 會這麼寫！

1. As a result of an increase in the pricing of our raw materials and production costs of our products, we are here to inform you of our decision to increase prices by 3% from January 1st 2017.
我們產品的原料和生產成本都提高了，因此在此通知您，我們已決定將我們的價格調高 3%，自 2017 年 1 月 1 日起生效。

2. We have been in production for over 10 years but not had a widespread price adjustment. Effective January 15, 2017, we'll implement a price increase of 5% across our whole range of products.
我們投入生產已超過 10 年了，但價格都還沒有大規模調整過。從 2017 年 1 月 15 日開始，我們所有產品的價格都將調漲 5%。

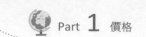

字彙 應用開口說：電話要這麼講！ Track 17

D ▶ Distributor 代理商　**M** ▶ Manufacturer 廠商

D ▶ We noted from your newsletter that you'll have a price increase next year, right?

代理商 ▶ 我們看到您們的電子報上頭說到明年要漲價，是嗎？

M ▶ Yes! Due to increasing raw material and packaging costs, we'll increase our prices for a majority of our antibodies.

廠商 ▶ 是的！因為原料和包裝成本都增加了，所以我們將會對多數的抗體進行價格調整。

D ▶ Will there be a significant increase?

代理商 ▶ 漲幅會很大嗎？

M ▶ No, it's just a minor adjustment. It'll be 3% approximately.

廠商 ▶ 不會的，只有些微的調整，大約是漲個 3%。

D ▶ I see! How about A101 reagents? Will this line of products also have a price rise?

代理商 ▶ 瞭解！那 A101 試劑呢？這類產品也會漲價嗎？

M ▶ No, it's unaffected by this price increase and will remain at the current prices until the end of 2017.

廠商 ▶ 不會，這類產品不會調價，到 2017 年年底都還會維持現在的價格。

D ▶ That's great. I think, for antibodies, we'll stock up on ourhigh demand items before price change takes effect!

代理商 ▶ 太棒了！對於抗體的部分，我想我們會針對需要量高的品項，在價格調整前先備些貨。

M ▶ Yeah! That's exactly what we suggest to our customers!

廠商 ▶ 對！這就是我建議我們客戶的做法呢！

 Track 18

字字 計較說分明

adjustment [ə`dʒʌstmənt] *n.* 調整

例 The purpose of this letter is to provide you with an advance notice of a price adjustment on certain products for 2017.

這封信是要來預先通知您某些產品在 2017 年會有價格上的調整。

相關字 adjust *[ə`dʒʌst]* *v.* 調整

---

approximately [ə`prɑksəmɪtlɪ] *adv.* 大概

例 Unfortunately, we don't have this product in stock. It will take approximately 10 working days to be ready.

不過,這項產品目前沒現貨,約要十個工作天後才可供貨。

---

effect [ɪ`fɛkt] *n.* 效力

例 New prices will come into effect next month, so you have until the end of this month to purchase our products at their current prices.

新價格將於下個月生效,因此,到這個月底前,您還能以目前的價格來訂購我們的產品。

相關字 effective *[ɪ`fɛktɪv]* *adj.* 生效的

---

increase [`ɪnkris] *n.* 增加；[ɪn`kris] *v.* 增加

例 As a follow-up to the e-mail notice sent in September, we will be implementing a rate increase on January 1, 2017.

繼九月時預先寄發 e-mail 通知之後，我們將在 2017 年一月一日調漲費率。

majority [mə`dʒɔrətɪ] *n.* 大多數

例 I have attached our 2017 distributor price list for you. There have been a few changes but the majority of products have remained the same price.

附上我們 2017 年的價格表給您，有一些變動，不過大多數的產品都還是維持一樣的價格。

相關字 major [`medʒɚ] *adj.* 較大的、較多的

反義字 minority [maɪ`nɔrətɪ] *n.* 少數

significantly [sɪg`nɪfəkəntlɪ] *adv.* 顯著地

例 As we have made an exception in order to win this order and significantly lowered our margin, we ask that you do the same.

為了贏得這個訂單，我們以特例處理，也大幅降低了利潤，因此我們要求您也比照辦理。

1-7 計算報價 Price Calculation

There will be a handling **fee**...

🌐 **字彙 導覽解說**

○ Track 19

　　產品之外還有些什麼費用呢？產品成本是廠商報價的重點，但除了產品之外，若沒問清楚相關費用有哪些，那等收到 Invoice 時，可能就是你下巴掉下來的時候呢！我們在這來統整一下，依據不同的交貨條件，來分層看看究竟有哪些費用囉！

EXW 出廠價
包裝費（Packaging fee / charge）
處理手續費（Handling fee / charge）
文件費（Documentation fee / charge）
銀行手續費（Bank fee / charge）
內陸運費（Inland shipping fee / charge）
FOB 船上交貨價／FCA 運送人交貨價
出口運費（Shipping fee / charge、freight）
CPT 運費付訖交貨價

保險費（Insurance）
CIP 運保費付訖交貨價

📧 字彙 應用搶先看：E-mail 會這麼寫！

1. Please note that this product is a limited quantity dangerous item. To ship this product internationally, <u>there will be an $80 handling fee.</u>

   要請您注意一點，這項產品屬於限制數量的危險品項，要辦理出口則須收取$80 的處理手續費。

2. If you choose to ship via FedEx freight collect, you'll be responsible for the freight charges.

   若您選擇 FedEx 運費到付的方式來出貨，那麼運費就是由您來負擔。

3. We have checked on the bank charges we have paid so far and it has varied between USD 18.00 to 35.00.

   我們查了先前付過的銀行手續費，發現金額從 USD 18.00 到 35.00 都有。

字彙 應用開口說：電話要這麼講！ Track 20

M ▶ Manufacturer 廠商　　**C** ▶ Customer客戶

M ▶ Hi, I'm calling to check whether you've received my e-mail and got the link to the product information.

廠商 ▶ 嗨！我想來跟您確認一下您有沒有收到我的e-mail，有看到產品資料連結了嗎？

C ▶ Yeah! I did. We know you offered an ex-works price. Please also tell me how much your shipping and handling fee is.

客戶 ▶ 有的！我有收到了。我們知道您的報價是出廠價，也請告訴我出貨處理費的金額是多少。

M ▶ Normally, it's $50, but your inquired product needs to be shipped on dry ice, so there will be a handling charge for the dry ice and special shipping box of $ 80.

廠商 ▶ 通常是$50，不過您詢問的產品得要用乾冰出貨，所以要收乾冰和特殊出貨箱子的處理手續費，金額是$80。

C ▶ Okay. Are there any other fees?

客戶 ▶ 好的，有任何其他的費用嗎？

M ▶ Will you pay by bank wire transfer? If yes, then an additional $20 bank charge will be added.

廠商 ▶ 您們會是用銀行匯款來付款嗎？如果是的話，那就還要加收$20的銀行手續費。

C ▶ Got it. Will you e-mail me your official quote including all related fees?

客戶 ▶ 瞭解，請問您會 e-mail 給我加計了所有相關費用的正式報價單嗎？

M ▶ Not a problem! I'll do it right away!

廠商 ▶ 沒問題，我會馬上發給您！

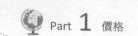 字字 計較說分明

charge [tʃɑrdʒ]　*n.*　費用；*v.*　收費

例 The buyer is responsible for any associated bank charges on all overseas transactions.

買方要負擔所有海外交易所產生的任何相關銀行費用。

---

cost [kɔst]　*n.*　成本、費用；　*v.*　花費

例 Due to high production costs, we are not able to match the competitor's pricing.

因為生產成本高，我們無法降至跟競爭者相同的價格水準。

---

fare [fɛr]　*n.*　車資、船費

例 Bus and train fare increases have come into effect, with prices rising by more than three times the rate of inflation.

公車與地鐵車資調漲今已生效，其價格調漲幅度比通貨膨脹率還大上三倍有餘。

---

fee [fi]　*n.*　費用、酬金

例 Payments via credit card mean additional work for us and therefore we may need to charge a handling fee of USD 30.00.

以信用卡付款對我們來說需要額外的處理作業，因此，我們

可能會要收取 USD 30.00 的手續費。

expense [ɪk`spɛns]　*n.*　費用

例 We'll send 100 free catalogs to our distributors, but each distributor is responsible for shipping expenses.

我們會寄送 100 份免費型錄給我們的代理商，但運費得由各個代理商來負擔。

相關字 expend *[ɪk`spɛnd]*　*v.*　消費、花費（時間、精力等）；expenditure *[ɪk`spɛndɪtʃɚ]*　*n.*　消費、支出

surcharge [`sɝˌtʃɑrdʒ]　*v.*　加收；　*n.*　額外費用

例 Payment by credit card is also acceptable, but we may add a 3% surcharge for the processing fee for credit card transactions.

我們也可接受信用卡付款，這部分的交易會要加收 3 ％ 的處理費。

1-8 價格結構 Price Structure

The transfer price will be...

 Track 22

字彙 導覽解說

　　從原廠定價到最後報給客戶／使用者的銷售價格中間，若還有個代理商的存在，那就會生出幾個不同層級與說法的價格囉！請各位看倌看了～

List price 定價
↓
Distributor price 代理商價格 Discounted price（Disc. price）折扣後價格 Transfer price 移轉價格
↓
Landed cost 落地成本 貨品到達代理商處之前的所有成本： 產品成本＋運費＋報關費＋稅負等成本
↓
End user price 最終使用者／客戶價格 （總成本 Total Cost＋利潤 Profit、Margin）

Part 1 價格

字彙 應用搶先看：E-mail 會這麼寫！

1. We ask that a distributor take a very small margin (3%) to process this kind of projects as we are also cutting our margin to accommodate key customers. <u>The transfer price to you this time will be $1,200 per set while the end user price needs to be $1,290 per set.</u> Please let us know if you accept this request.

對於這類案子，我們要求代理商將利潤率降到很低（3％）來做，因為我們也同時降低了利潤率來配合重要客戶的要求。<u>我們這次給您的移轉價格會是每組$1,200，而您給客戶的價格須為每組$1,290</u>，請告知您是否接受這樣的要求。

2. Attached please find the distributor price list in EUR. On the mentioned list prices you will get a 50% discount (these are all transfer prices without any further discount).

在此附上歐元的代理商價格表，就所列出的定價，您們可享50％的折扣（這些皆為移轉價格，不再有任何額外的折扣）。

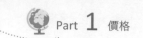
字彙 應用開口說：電話要這麼講！   Track 23

M▶ Manufacturer 廠商   D▶ Distributor 代理商

M▶ As our official distributor, we could offer you 20% distributor discount off list price.

廠商▶ 做為我們的正式代理商，我們可給您定價的20%的代理商折扣。

D▶ As you know, we're competing with the ACE Company and they always offer extremely low end-user prices. So could you support us by giving us 30% off for one kit?

代理商▶ 您知道我們是跟艾斯公司競爭，而他們報給客戶的價格都是非常地低，所以，請問您能給我們一組的折扣給到 30％嗎？

M▶ It's a large discount! Hmm... in order to provide competitive pricing, we could approve another 8% discount and we ask that you will decrease your margin as well.

廠商▶ 這折扣很大耶！嗯……，為了要給個有競爭力的價格，我們同意再多給8％的折扣，而同時您也要調降您的利潤率。

D▶ We'll do that! Even our offer will be close to our landed cost, we'll try to accommodate and win over the order!

代理商▶ 我們會的！就算我們的報價都快跟我們的落地成本一樣了，我們還是會盡量配合，拿下訂單！

M▶ It's great to hear that! So we look forward to hearing goods news from you soon!

廠商▶ 很高興聽到您這麼說！那我們就等著盡快聽到您的好消息囉！

字字 計較說分明 Track 24

accommodate [əˋkɑməˌdet] *v.* 配合、通融

例 We're able to accommodate your request to supply the custom size of this product.

我們可以配合您的要求，提供這一項產品的訂製包裝。

相關字 accommodation *[əˌkɑməˋdeʃən]* *n.* 適應、住宿

---

approve [əˋpruv] *v.* 核准、贊同

例 To compete with other brands, we hope you will approve a 50% discount.

為了能與其他廠牌競爭，我們希望您能同意提供 50%的折扣。

相關字 approval *[əˋpruvl̩]* *n.* 批准、贊成

---

margin [ˋmɑrdʒɪn] *n.* 利潤、利潤率

例 We're significantly decreasing our margin in order to provide competitive pricing; therefore, we ask that your company does the same.

為了要給個具競爭力的價格，我們大幅調降了利潤，因此，我們要求您們公司也要這麼做。

相關字 marginal *[ˋmɑrdʒɪnl̩]* *adj.* 邊際的

markup [`mɑrkˌʌp]　*n.*　加成、漲價

例 Our end user pricing includes a fixed markup of 15%.

我們的最終使用者價格加計了 15%的固定加成。

---

profit [`prɑfɪt]　*n.*　利潤

例 When we issue larger discounts, we expect you to reduce the profit also to win customers.

當我們提供更大折扣時，我們希望您也能同樣調降利潤，以爭取客戶。

---

revenue [`rɛvəˌnju]　*n.*　收入、收益

例 Please provide more background information about your company, such as your headcount, sales revenue and growth rate.

請提供更多您公司背景的資訊，例如人數、銷售額與成長率。

1-9 報價單 Quote Sheet

Attached is our quotation...

報價單（Quote、Quotation）裡頭有好幾個不同區塊與項目名稱，若不識得，就不免犯上原廠已說明但你還提問的窘境！在此列出完整報價單應有的項目名稱，請您逐一細看囉！

1. Business details／商業明細

   收貨人明細：Ship to、Shipping address

   付款人明細：Bill to、Billing address

2. Product details／產品明細

   型號：Catalog no.、Product code、Item no.

   品名：Product name、Product description、Material description

   規格：Size、Specification

3. Price details／價格明細

   單價：Unit price；幣別：Currency；小計：Subtotal；稅：

Tax；總計：Total、Total amount、Grand total；手續費：
Handling fee

4. Terms and conditions／條件

付款條件：Payment terms

出貨條件：Shipping conditions、Shipping terms

5. Quote expiry date／報價單效期

到期日：Expiration date、Expiry、Quotation valid until

📧 字彙 應用搶先看：E-mail 會這麼寫！

1. Thank you for your inquiry for bulk sizes of Item # 1202.
   Attached is our quotation to your company. Please note
   that this quotation will expire on 04/23/17. If I can help with
   anything else, please just let me know.

   謝謝您發來產品# 1202 大包裝的詢價，在此附上我們給您公
   司的報價單，請注意此報價單的效期至 04/23/17 為止，若還
   有什麼需要我協助的地方，就請直接告訴我。

2. I have attached the quote. Please make sure to reference
   the quote no. on your PO in order to receive the right
   discount. 我已附上了報價單，下單時請您務必在訂單上標
   註報價單單號，以能拿到正確的折扣。

字彙 應用開口說：電話要這麼講！ Track 26

M▶ Manufacturer 廠商   D▶ Distributor 代理商

M▶ I am following up on our recent quotation for A1 System. Is your customer interested in placing the order?

廠商▶ 我想來問問我們最近給您 A1 系統報價的後續狀況，您客戶有想要下訂單了嗎？

D▶ Our customer is still evaluating and will probably make the purchasing decision next month.

代理商▶ 我們的客戶還在評估，可能下個月會決定這個採購案。

M▶ But our quotation is valid until the end of this month. Please try to ask your customer to order sooner.

廠商▶ 不過我們報價的效期只到這個月底，還有勞您請客戶快些下單。

D▶ Okay. I'll push our customer and provide any assistance required to get the order placed. By the way, when could

代理商▶ 好的，我會催催我們的客戶，也會盡力協助他們決案下單。對了，若您收到我們的訂單後，多久可出

you ship the goods after receiving our order?

貨呢？

M ▶ As stated under the "Terms and Conditions" on our quotation, the product will be shipped within 3 working days after receiving your order.

廠商 ▶ 就跟我們報價單裡頭「條件」項下所寫的一樣，我們是收到您訂單後三個工作天內可出貨。

D ▶ I see! Please wait for my good news!

代理商 ▶ 瞭解！那就請您等我的好消息囉！

 字字 計較說分明

 Track 27

description [dɪˋskrɪpʃən] *n.* 敘述

例 You can click the product image on our website and then scroll down for the full product description.

您可以點入網站上的產品圖片，然後往下拉，就可看到完整的產品名稱。

相關字 describe *[dɪˋskraɪb]* *v.* 敘述

搭配詞 Technical Description 技術說明書；Job Description 工作說明書

---

grand [grænd] *adj.* 全部的、總的

例 The grand total is the final price that must be paid.

總金額是要支付的最終價格。

---

reference [ˋrɛfərəns] *v.* 提及； *n.* 參考、參考文獻

例 Simply reference promo code: # 0925PA when placing your order and you'll get a free T-shirt.

下單時只要加註促銷碼 0925PA，就可得到一件免費的 T 恤。

---

specification [ˌspɛsəfəˋkeʃən] *n.* 規格、詳細計畫書 ⑲ spec.

例 There will be no changes to the manufacturing processes or established product specifications as a result of the relocation of our factory.

我們工廠搬遷並不會在製程上或在已建立的產品規格上有任何的變動。

相關字 specific [spɪˋsɪfɪk] *adj.* 特定的；specify [ˋspɛsəˌfaɪ] *v.* 指名、具體說明

....

subtotal [sʌbˋtotl] *n.* 小計

例 If your order subtotal is greater than US$ 1,000, you'll get a free sample kit.

如果您訂單的小計金額有超過 US$ 1,000，就可獲得一組免費的樣品。

....

terms [tɝms] *n.* 條款（用複數）、（協議上的）條件。= conditions、provisions

例 Please note that the payment terms are 30 days after the invoice date.

請注意付款條件為發票日後 30 天。

2-1 下單 Placing an Order

We'd like to **place** an **order** for...

字彙 導覽解說

終於談定了價格、出貨條件、付款條件等等細節，總算要來祭出訂單大禮啦！就讓我們來看看下單有哪些相關的字詞，也來看看所下的訂單又有分哪些種類囉！

1. 客戶下了單（place an order）、廠商接了單（receive an order）之後，廠商就要開始跑訂單處理（process）流程了，要跟客戶確認（confirm）訂單內容，而客戶也要看看有無要修改（modify、revise、amend），有無要追單（add to order），或者是有新狀況出現而要取消（cancel）訂單。

2. 依有無訂貨紀錄來看，訂單可分首次下單的訂單（initial order），以及從訂單紀錄（order history）中所叫出來，直接重下的訂單（repeat orders）。若依訂單的量或特殊性，則可分一般訂單（regular orders）、大量訂購的訂單（bulk orders）、特殊規格的訂製訂單（custom orders）。

![字彙 應用搶先看：E-mail 會這麼寫！]

1. We'd like to place an order for your Controller. Attached please find our Purchase Order. Please confirm and process the order for us. Also please e-mail your Proforma Invoice to me so that we could make payment to you by wire transfer.

   我們想要下單訂購您的控制器，在此附上訂購單，還請確認並替我們處理此訂單，也請 e-mail 形式發票給我，這樣我們才能安排用電匯來支付貨款給您。

2. Following our previous discussions, we are pleased to place our initial order to you for 10 kits of PY1202 Controller. The product details and our preferred shipping method are listed as follows. Please confirm the order and let us know the estimated shipping date.

   延續我們先前的討論，我們很高興要來跟您下我們的第一張訂單，訂購 10 組的 PY1202 控制器。在此列出產品明細以及我們想要的出貨方式，請您確認此訂單，並告知預估的出貨日。

Part 2 ｜ 訂單

字彙 應用開口說：電話要這麼講！ Track 29

D ▶ Distributor 代理商　M ▶ Manufacturer 廠商

D ▶ Hi, we've made a decision about purchasing your microscopes!

代理商 ▶ 嗨，我們已經決定要訂購您的顯微鏡了！

M ▶ Great! How many sets do you need?

廠商 ▶ 太棒了！您要訂多少組呢？

D ▶ We'd like to start with an initial order of 10 sets. If customers respond well to your microscopes, we'll then make repeat orders to you!

代理商 ▶ 第一次下單，我們想要訂個 10 組，如果客戶對您顯微鏡的反應不錯，那我們之後就會重覆下單囉！

M ▶ I'm glad to hear that! If you place a bulk order, I could lower the price for you!

廠商 ▶ 很高興聽到您這麼說！如果您要一次下個大單，那我就會降價給您！

D ▶ I'm also hoping to give you a big order! For these 10 sets,

代理商 ▶ 我也希望能給您一個大單呢！那對我們要訂的

when will they be shipped at the soonest?

這 10 組，請問最快什麼時候可以出貨呢？

M ▶ We could have them ready in 3 working days after receiving your order.

廠商 ▶ 我們可在接單後三天將貨準備好。

D ▶ That's fine. I'll e-mail you our order later today!

代理商 ▶ 那可以，今天稍晚我就會 e-mail 給您我們的訂單！

Track 30

bulk [bʌlk]　*adj.*　大量的、大批的、散裝的

例 This product is available in 3 sizes, with bulk discounts available.

這個產品有三種規格可供應，有提供量大的折扣。

其他字義　*n.*　體積、容積、大塊、大部份

---

initial [ɪˋnɪʃəl]　*adj.*　最初的

例 Thank you for your added items. These have been included in your initial order.

謝謝您追加的品項，這些品項都已加進您最初的訂單了。

相關字 initiate *[ɪˋnɪʃɪˏet]*　*v.*　開始、創始

---

order [ˋɔrdɚ]　*n.*　訂單；　*v.*　訂購

例 Please acknowledge receipt and acceptance of this order by returning the copy duly signed.

請簽名回傳訂單副本，以表示收到並接受此訂單。

其他字義　*n.*　次序、整齊、命令；　*v.*　整理、安排、命令

---

place [ples]　*v.*　開出（訂單）

例 Please place your formal PO when you are ready and we will process it immediately.

請您準備好之後，開立正式的訂購單給我們，我們會立即處理。

---

preferred [prɪ`fɝd]　*adj.*　優先的、更好的

例 To make payments, by our preferred method of bank transfer, our bank details are included on our invoices.

在付款方面，我們偏好的方式為銀行匯款，發票上有列出我們的銀行資料。

相關字 prefer *[prɪ`fɝ]*　*v.*　寧可、寧願（選擇）、更喜歡

---

process [`prɑsɛs]　*v.*　處理、加工

例 Any orders received after Thursday will be processed and shipped the following week.

對於星期四之後才收到的任何訂單，都只能等到下一週才能處理及出貨。

其他字義　*n.*　過程、步驟、程序

Part 2 ｜訂單

2-2 改用網路下單
Changing to Order Online
Please consider ordering online...

字彙 導覽解說

　　許多廠商都建置了線上下單（Online ordering）的系統，有的廠商乾脆規定只接受線上下單，而有的廠商則是不管你怎麼下單都會受理，但還是會說明一下，以吸引你改用網路下單囉！

1. **好處在此**：對下單者來說，網路下單有幾個好處，例如可直接從網路上看到價格（Pricing）和產品的現貨狀況（Availability status），下單後也可直接在線上追蹤訂單狀況（track order status），之後還可直接叫出、取回（retrieve）訂單的歷史紀錄，以再次下單（re-order from order history）。

2. **設立帳戶**：要線上下單的先決條件就是要先登記（Register）、設立新帳戶（Create / Set up a new account），申請後就可登入（Login）帳戶，建立、編輯（Edit）帳戶裡的出貨地址（Shipping address）、帳單地

址（Billing address）、出貨方式（Shipping method）及付款方式（Payment method）。

✉ 字彙 應用搶先看：E-mail 會這麼寫！

1. Please register on our website, login and visit the 'My Account' page to complete credit account form and email it to us along with a blank copy of your company headed paper. Once your account has been set up, we will advise you and you will be able to place online orders.

   請先在網站上登記，登入後請到「我的帳戶」填寫信用帳戶格式，再連同有您公司抬頭的空白信紙一起 e-mail 給我們。等您的帳戶建立了之後，我們會通知您，您就可以線上下單了。

2. Please consider ordering online. It allows you to track the status and shipment of your order, re-order from your order history and retrieve application news relevant to the ordered products.

   請考慮線上下單的方式，它可讓您追蹤訂單的狀況與出貨情形，也可從歷史訂單中直接重新訂單，還能直接取得所訂產品的相關應用資訊。

Part 2 訂單

字彙 應用開口說：電話要這麼講！ Track 32

M▶ Manufacturer 廠商　C▶ Customer 客戶

M▶ I received your e-mail earlier today notifying us of your credit card details. Unfortunately, due to security issues we are not able to accept or process credit card transactions via e-mail.

廠商▶ 我稍早收到了您的 e-mail，通知我們您的信用卡明細，不過，基於安全因素，我們無法透過 e-mail 來處理信用卡交易耶！

C▶ So... Could I tell you the card details on the phone right now?

客戶▶ 那麼……，我現在可以在電話上告訴您信用卡資料嗎？

M▶ Since you want to make payments by credit card, we recommend you place orders through our online web store.

廠商▶ 既然您要用信用卡付款，我們建議您在我們的線上網路商店上下單訂購喔！

C▶ Could you tell me more about how to order online?

客戶▶ 那能不能請您跟我說一下要怎麼樣線上下單呢？

M ▶ Sure! You can simply set up an account by entering your e-mail address, choose "I am a new customer" and enter a password.Then you can start to order and pay online!

C ▶ Sounds so easy! I'll give it a try right away!

廠商 ▶ 當然可以！您只要輸入您的 e-mail 地址，點選「我是新客戶」，再輸入密碼，就可建立帳戶了，然後您就可以開始在線上下單、付款囉！

客戶 ▶ 聽起來很容易呢！我馬上就來試試！

 字字 計較說分明

access [`æksɛs] *v.* 進入、接近、（電腦）取出（資料）

例 If you have any difficulty accessing our website resources, please feel free to contact me.

若您無法取得我們網站上的資源訊息，請隨時與我聯絡。

---

register [`rɛdʒɪstɚ] *v.* 登記

例 You're invited to attend our web seminar. Please register soon before it's too late.

我們邀請您參加我們的網路研討會，還請盡早登記，以免向隅。

---

retrieve [rɪ`triv] *v.* 取回、（電腦）擷取（資料）

例 The only other fees associated would be the customs fees which you are responsible for when retrieving the product.

唯一有關的其他費用就是當您要取回貨物時所要負擔的關稅了。

---

security [sɪ`kjʊrətɪ] *n.* 安全、防護

例 Please be aware that due to security concerns, we ask customers not to send credit card details via e-mail or fax.

請注意，基於安全考量，我們要求客戶不要用 e-mail 或傳真來發送信用卡明細。

---

set up [ˋsɛtˏʌp] *verb. ph.* 建立

例 If you do not have an online account set up yet, please register and then I will also set the Distributor discount to your account.

若是您還沒建立線上帳戶，那就請您登記，然後我也會將您的帳戶設定為適用代理商折扣。

---

switch [swɪtʃ] *v.* *n.* 轉換、調換

例 All our credit card customers have switched to ordering online so far.

目前我們所有的信用卡客戶都已改為線上下單了。

---

transaction [trænˋzækʃən] *n.* 交易

例 The transaction ID for this refund is listed below. Please let me know if you have any questions.

在此將這次退款的交易識別碼列出如下，如有任何問題，再請告訴我。

Part 2 訂單

2-3 網路下單程序
Online Ordering Procedure

Browse through the product catalogue...

🌐 **字彙 導覽解說**

　　選擇了網路下單，從開始選產品到最後結帳下單，各家廠商設計的流程都差不多，線上要求的資訊也大致相同！我們現在就來瀏覽一次線上下單的必經要點囉！

1. 首要重點當然是要瀏覽（browse）、搜尋（search）想訂的產品，可透過產品導覽連結（navigation link）來找，確定後就可點入（click）、選擇（select、choose）產品，從下拉選單（dropdown menu）中選取規格與數量，下單，接著就會被引導（directed）到購物車或購物籃（shopping cart、trolley、basket）的畫面囉！

2. 若還有要再選取的品項，那就請點選繼續購物（continue shopping），若產品已選取完畢，那就進行結帳（proceed to checkout）囉！

3. 要完成結帳程序（complete checkout process），一定會有
這些步驟，會要你一步步提供資訊並確認，走完程序就完成
下單囉：

a) 填寫出貨資訊（shipping info）與發票資訊（billing info）

b) 付款（Payment）

c) 檢查後下單（Review and place an order）

d) 訂單確認（Confirmation of order）

字彙 應用搶先看：E-mail 會這麼寫！

1. Browse through the product catalogue.
瀏覽產品型錄。

2. Add items to your shopping cart by clicking the "buy"
button next to your desired product. You are then directed
to the shopping cart page.
點選您所要產品旁的「購買」按鍵，加入購物車，則會引導
您至購物車的頁面。

3. You can select to proceed to checkout, alternatively you
can choose to continue shopping. If you select to go to
checkout, you will be directed to the shipping info page.
您可選擇進行結帳，也可選擇繼續購物。若您選擇結帳，則
會引導您至出貨資訊的頁面。

Part 2 │ 訂單

字彙 應用開口說：電話要這麼講！ Track 35

C ▶ Customer 客戶　　**M** ▶ Manufacturer 廠商

C ▶ I had difficulty placing my order on your website. Could you help me?

客戶 ▶ 我在您們網站下單有碰到問題，您能幫我嗎？

M ▶ Sure! Please tell me what your problem is.

廠商 ▶ 當然可以！請告訴我是什麼問題。

C ▶ I couldn't find the product I desire to order...

客戶 ▶ 我找不到我要訂的產品在哪裡……。

M ▶ Okay. Are you online now?

廠商 ▶ 好的，您現在在線上嗎？

C ▶ Yes!

客戶 ▶ 是的！

M ▶ Great! You can browse our full range using the top navigation bar where all the products are categorized. Then

廠商 ▶ 很好！您可以從頁面最上方的導覽列來瀏覽我們已分類好的所有產品。請選擇您想要產品的產品種類，

please select the product group of the product you desired, and the relevant items will be displayed on screen and you can click on that item to display the product details and prices.

C ▶ Wait a moment... Yeah! I see the item I want!

M ▶ Excellent! Then you can select the quantity you require and click the 'Add to Basket' button. The page will be refreshed and your item will appear in your shopping basket.

C ▶ Got it! Thanks a lot!

這樣它相關的品項就都會出現在畫面中，然後請您點選您要的產品，接著就會出現那一項產品的明細跟價格了。

客戶 ▶等一下……，有了！我有看到我要的產品了。

廠商 ▶太棒了！接著您可以選擇您要的數量，點「加入購物籃」按鍵，頁面就會更新，而您要的品項就會顯現在購物籃中囉！

客戶 ▶了解了，多謝！

Part 2 訂單

字字 計較說分明

browse [braʊz]　*v.*　瀏覽

例 If you need promotional flyers, you can simply click this link and browse through all our data.

若是您有要促銷文宣,您只需要點此連結,瀏覽我們所有的資料。

其他字義 （動物）吃（葉或嫩枝）

---

click [klɪk]　*v.*　滑鼠點擊、發出喀擦聲

例 Just to show you how easy the ordering process is, we have created a video which might be helpful. Please click the icon below to see the video.

就是為了要讓您看看訂單程序有多麼簡單,我們製作了一段影片,可能對您有幫助。請點下列的圖示來看這段影片。

---

direct [dəˋrɛkt]　*v.*　給……指路、指向

例 This Invoice is for your payment reference. Any questions regarding the order should be directed to customer service.

這份 Invoice 是供您付款參照用,若您有關於這筆訂單的任何問題,請向客戶服務人員提出詢問。

display [dɪˋsple] *v.* 顯示、陳列

例 The order is scheduled to be shipped on or before the date displayed above.

這筆訂單預計在上方所列的出貨日當天或之前安排寄出。

navigation [͵nævəˋgeʃən] *n.* 導覽、導航

例 The "products tab" located on the homepage has been given a makeover for more organized navigation.

在首頁裡的「產品標籤」已重新設計，使得在導覽上更有組織性可循。

proceed [prəˋsid] *v.* 進行

例 Please let me know how you would like to proceed with the order.

請告訴我您要如何進行此訂單。

Part 2 ｜訂單

2-4 訂貨確認
Order Confirmation

Please find attached your Order **Acknowledgment**.

 Track 37

　　廠商收到訂單後，會出具一份文件，列出所有訂單相關訊息，以與買方做最後確認，避免有任何的失誤與誤解。這份文件有好些個不同的稱號，有小異，但基本上是大同的喔！

1. 訂貨確認單的名稱

　　- Order Confirmation／訂貨確認單

　　- Sales Order／銷售訂單

　　- Order Acknowledgement／訂單確認單

　　- Sales Acknowledgement／銷售確認單

　　- P.O. Confirmation／採購訂單確認單

　　- Confirmation／確認單

2. 收到廠商來的訂貨確認單資訊後，有幾個動作要做，首先要好好檢查，若有發現任何與你下單內容與條件不符之處（discrepancy），就得立即寫回反應（advise immediately

by return e-mail），要求修正（correct、rectify、revise），等所有大小要點都確認無誤後，有的廠商還會再要求 e-mail 回覆確認或簽名（sign）確認。

✉ 字彙 應用搶先看：E-mail 會這麼寫！

1. Please find attached your Order Acknowledgment for PO No. 1202. The Order Acknowledgment confirms the shipping date and related details. Kindly please look over this to ensure accuracy. Should you have any questions or queries, please do not hesitate to contact me.

   請見您訂購單單號 1202 的訂貨確認單如附，此確認單上會確認出貨日期及其他明細，請逐一審閱，以確保正確無誤。若您有任何的問題，請儘管與我聯絡。

2. Please find attached our Sales Acknowledgement in relation to your Purchase Order number referenced. Please check the Acknowledgement and in the event of any discrepancies, advise us immediately by return e-mail.

   附上我們對您上述單號之訂購單的銷售確認單，請檢查一下此確認單，如有任何不符之處，還請立即以 e-mail 告訴我們。

字彙 應用開口說：電話要這麼講！ Track 38

M▶ Manufacturer 廠商　C▶ Customer 客戶

M▶ Hi, I sent our Sales Order to you last week. I haven't received any further news from you. Did you receive it?

廠商▶ 嗨，我上星期有發了銷售訂單給您，但我還沒聽到您的回音，請問您有收到嗎？

C▶ Yeah, I did. But I've been expecting to receive the shipping notification from you... So, do you need to get our confirmation before shipment?

客戶▶ 有的，我有收到，不過我是在等您發來出貨通知耶……，所以，您要我們做確認後才出貨，是嗎？

M▶ Correct. As stated on our Sales Orders, we are requiring all of them to be approved before shipping. Without those confirmations, orders will be held.

廠商▶ 沒錯，我們在銷售訂單上有寫說所有訂單都得核准後才會出貨，若是沒有確認，訂單就會暫停處理。

C ▶ I didn't notice that. Sorry. Thanks for calling to remind me. I'll sign it immediately and e-mail it back to you!

客戶▶ 我沒注意到這點，抱歉，也謝謝您打來提醒我，我會馬上簽名，再回傳給您！

M ▶ If we could receive it within the next 2 hours, the order could be shipped out today.

廠商▶ 若是我們可以在 2 小時之內收到您回傳的訂單，那我們今天就可出貨。

C ▶ Great to hear that! Thanks!

客戶▶ 太棒了！謝謝！

Part 2 訂單

 Track 39

acknowledgement [əkˋnɑlɪdʒmənt]　*n.*　確認通知

例 Please see the attached order acknowledgment for order # 0925. The goods will be shipped today as requested.

請見訂單單號 0925 的訂貨確認單如附，我們會依您要求，在今天出貨。

其他字義 承認、致謝

---

accurate [ˋækjərɪt]　*adj.*　準確的、精確的

例 All International Orders must be confirmed as accurate before shipping by sending an email to us.

所有國際訂單皆須以 e-mail 回覆確認正確無誤後，我們才會出貨。

相關字 accuracy [ˋækjərəsɪ]　*v.*　正確、準確

---

conform [kənˋfɔrm]　*v.*　符合

例 We only accept returns where goods are faulty or where they do not conform to the order.

我們只接受貨物有瑕疵或與訂單不符的退貨。

其他字義 遵照、順從

discrepancy [dɪ`skrɛpənsɪ] *n.* 不符、不一致

例 Please kindly check the OC details as attached and let me know immediately if there is any discrepancy.

請檢查附件的訂貨確認單明細，若有任何不符之處，還請立刻告訴我。

hold [hold] *v.* 扣留

例 Please note that without receiving confirmations by return e-mail, all orders will be held and not processed.

請注意，若我們沒有收到 e-mail 回覆確認，所有的訂單都會扣留著不處理。

搭配詞 hold up *v. ph.* 延遲、耽擱

signature [`sɪgnətʃɚ] *n.* 簽名

例 If you go all the way to the bottom of the form, it states "Approved By" and that is where we need your approval signature.

若您往表格最下方看，有一處寫著「核准人」，那就是我們需要您核簽的地方。

相關字 sign *[saɪn]* *v.* 簽名； *v.* 記號、標誌

2-5 修改訂單
Order Modification

We have to **adjust** the quantity of our order...

下了訂單後，雖說是定案了、締結了個承諾，但總是有無法預知的新狀況出現，逼得客戶不得不來修改訂單（change an order）。我們就來看看怎麼說「改」，為何而「改」囉！

1. 說到「修改」，那可選用的英文字可就多了，有 amend、revise、modify、alter，也會說要更正（correct）或要調整（adjust）。

2. 在數量的修改上，就有說來可大聲的加量（add、increase、raise），也有令人不太好意思啟齒的減量（decrease、reduce），不過，再怎麼不好意思，也都比要說取消（cancel、call off）訂單自在些！

3. 要修改訂單的理由百百種，理由正當者可能像是採購案延期（delayed、postponed、deferred、set back）、受了耽擱（held up），甚至是計畫暫停（paused）或中止

（suspended）。也有些理由說來不好意思，像是因經手人員的疏忽（oversight），有可能要買×1，卻出現筆誤（clerical error）或打錯字（typo），寫成了×11 哩！

字彙 應用搶先看：E-mail 會這麼寫！

1. We did place our official order to you but our customer's project is postponed to a later date and therefore we have to adjust the time scale and quantity of our order as follows. We appreciate if you could confirm your acceptance at your earliest convenience.

我們有下了正式訂單給您，但是我們客戶的案子往後延了，所以我們得調整我們訂單的時間排程和數量，請見明細如下，若您能盡快跟我們確認接受此修改，我們將會很感激。

2. We'd like to decrease the quantity of our order if at all possible. This is due to the fact that our customer's experiment was delayed, so his exact demand at this stage will be lower than the ordered quantity. Please confirm the order change.

如果可以的話，我們想要減少我們所訂的數量，因為我們客戶的實驗有延遲，因此他現階段的實際需求會比訂購量來得少。還請您確認此訂單變更。

Part 2 訂單

 **字彙** 應用開口說：電話要這麼講！ Track 41

D ▶ Distributor 代理商　M ▶ Manufacturer 廠商

D ▶ Hello, have you shipped out our order already?

代理商 ▶ 哈囉，請問我們的訂單已經出了嗎？

M ▶ Not yet! We're hoping to get it ready for shipping this afternoon.

廠商 ▶ 還沒呢！我們希望今天下午貨可準備好寄出。

D ▶ Oh, No! First, please accept my apologies. I noted from your Order Acknowledgement that I had a typo in the order. I wanted to order "1" kit but typed "11" by oversight!

代理商 ▶ 喔，不！請先接受我的道歉，我看到你的訂貨確認單，才發現我訂單的數量打錯了，我要打的是「1」，結果不小心打成「11」了！

M ▶ Are you sure it's a typo? I was excited to see you ordered such a big quantity.

廠商 ▶ 你確定是打錯嗎？看到你下的這個大單，我還很興奮耶！

D ▶ Come on! Don't make fun of me! Please do me a favor and correct the quantity and e-mail me the revised Order Acknowledgement.

代理商 ▶ 拜託！不要取笑我啦！請你幫忙一下，修正訂貨的量，再請將修改的訂貨確認單 e-mail 給我。

M ▶ I could do that for you because the kits are not packed yet.

廠商 ▶ 我可以為你這麼做，因為這些貨也都還沒打包。

D ▶ Thanks, my dear friend!

代理商 ▶ 謝謝你了，我親愛的朋友！

 字字 計較說分明 Track 42

adjust [ə`dʒʌst] *v.* 調整、調節、適應

例 Once you have reviewed the catalog, please let me know as soon as possible about the requested quantities you'd like to adjust.

等您看過這份型錄之後，請盡快告訴我您是否有要調整您所要的數量。

---

amend [ə`mend] *v.* 修改

例 Should you wish to amend your selection, simply click on the 'Basket' where you will have the opportunity to remove or amend the quantity of the product selected.

若您要修改所選內容，您只要點進「購物籃」，就可移除或修改所選產品的數量。

---

cancel [`kænsl] *v.* 取消

例 The reason that we delayed the delivery was because we were supposed to have maintenance on our shipping system. But, that was cancelled, so we can ship it for you today instead.

我們延遲出貨的原因是因為我們本來應該要做出貨系統維護，但取消了，所以我們今天就可出貨給您們。

postpone [post`pon] *v.* 延期

例 Due to technical difficulties, we will not be able to ship your package today and will postpone the delivery date.

因為技術上遇到困難，我們今天沒辦法出貨，到貨日也會往後延。

revise [rɪ`vaɪz] *v.* 修改

例 Please inform specifically what packaging you would like and I can supply a revised quote.

請明確地告知您所要的是哪一種包裝，這樣我才能修改報價單給您。

suspend [sə`spɛnd] *v.* 中止

例 Authentication of this transaction failed and the transaction has been suspended. Please try again using a different credit card.

此交易驗證失敗，因此交易已中止，請以別張信用卡再試一次。

Part 2 │訂單

2-6 訂製訂單 Custom Order

If you'd like to request a **custom** order...

字彙 導覽解說

客戶若要向廠商訂購訂製的產品，那麼訂製的特殊規格事前務必溝通好，廠商也會要求客戶將訂製內容明確列出，而在付款上也可能會有不同於一般訂單的條件喔！

1. 訂製產品（custom product）在規格（specifications）上會有特殊的要求（special requirements），通常廠商會請客戶填寫規格表（Specification Form），以確保清楚溝通、有憑有據。

2. 訂製訂單（custom order）的交貨準備期（lead time）會較長，在付款條件上，有的廠商也會要求一定比例的預付貨款（advance payment、upfront payment）。而一旦下單後，通常就不會接受再經修改（amended）或額外的（additional）規格要求，另外，也因為是為客戶量身訂做，自然也不會接受任何的反悔，無法取消訂單。

字彙 應用搶先看：E-mail 會這麼寫！

1. If you'd like to request a custom order, please get in touch using the Specification Form below. I'll contact you as soon as possible to discuss your requirements, and to agree on an estimated price and timescale.

   如果您想要下訂製訂單，就請您發來如下的規格表，跟我們連絡，我會盡快跟您連絡，跟您討論您的需求，也跟您談談您可接受的估價與時間排程。

2. As your inquiry qualifies as a custom order, I will need you to fill out the Specification Form attached. Once I receive the completed form, I will be able review the request to develop a formal and final quote.

   您的詢價屬於訂製訂單的範圍，請您填寫附件的規格表，等我收到您填寫完整的表格後，我就可看看您的要求內容，再出具正式與底定的報價單給您。

Part 2 ｜訂單

字彙 應用開口說：電話要這麼講！ Track 44

C ▶ Customer 客戶　M ▶ Manufacturer 廠商

C ▶ Did you receive the custom order that we sent yesterday?

客戶 ▶ 請問您有收到我們昨天發的訂製訂單嗎？

M ▶ Yes, we did. Our Production Manager confirms that this product will be prepared according to the specifications detailed in your order and will have passed our standard quality control procedures before release.

廠商 ▶ 是的，我們有收到。我們的生產經理有確認了貨可以依照您訂單中所列的規格來做，也會等貨通過了我們的標準品質管理程序後再放行。

C ▶ Thanks for letting me know about this! By the way, I'd like to check one point with you. What if we need to amend a certain spec.? Do you have any requirements on this?

客戶 ▶ 謝謝您告訴我這些消息！對了，我也想跟您問一件事，如果我們有要修改某項規格，您會怎麼處理？有什麼相關要求嗎？

M ▶ Sorry, but we cannot accept any amended or additional specifications subsequent to your acceptance of our order confirmation.

廠商 ▶ 這點要跟您說抱歉了，在您對我們的訂貨確認單做確認之後，我們就不接受任何修改或新增的規格了。

C ▶ Got it! If we do have any spec. to add to the order, we'll inform you asap.

客戶 ▶ 瞭解！若是我們有要增加任何的規格，我們會盡快告訴您。

Part 2 訂單

 Track 45

acceptance [ək`sɛptəns]　*n.*　接受

例 The Contract shall come into effect upon receipt of a signed order form or written acceptance.

這份合約會在收到您簽回訂單或是書面表示接受後生效。

---

advance [əd`væns]　*adj.*　預先的

例 Advance payment is required prior to the commencement of production. Once the payment is received, we'll process your order right away.

開始生產前，須預先付清貨款，等我們一收到貨款，就會立即開始處理訂單。

---

custom [`kʌstəm]　*adj.*　訂製的

例 For custom synthesis orders, a 30% advance payment is needed to initiate the order.

對於訂製合成的訂單，您得先行支付 30%的貨款，之後我們才會開始處理訂單。

其他字義　*n.*　海關、習俗

相關字 customize [`kʌstəm͵aɪz]　*v.*　訂做

---

indicate [`ɪndəˌket]　*v.*　指出、指示

例 Please make sure that you indicate the products and exact quantity that your customer will require on the custom specification form.

請務必在訂製規格表上列明您客戶所要的產品與確實的數量。

---

release [rɪ`lis]　*n. v.*　放出、釋放、發行

例 Your inquired product is out of stock. We expect a new release in June. Please let me know whether your customer is willing to wait or not.

您所詢的產品並沒有現貨，我們預期六月可有新批推出，請告知您的客戶是否願意等。

---

requirement [rɪ`kwaɪrmənt]　*n.*　要求、必要條件

例 We are confident that we can actually make the product that meets your specification requirements.

我們有信心可以確實生產符合您規格要求的產品。

Part 2 ｜訂單

3-1 出貨方式
Shipping Method

You can choose from **express**, sea and air freight...

字彙 導覽解說

　　國際貿易的出貨方式（Mode of Shipment、Shipping Method）種類多不多呢？若要分大類來看，就只海運與空運兩種罷了，不過在海空運大類裡，到了安排出貨（arrange / coordinate shipments）時，倒也還有這有那，有好些方式可供選擇。現在就讓我們來看看有哪些選項囉！

1. 出貨方式分有空運（air freight）與海運（sea freight）兩種。而就空中的速度來說，最快的會是走快遞（express、courier）出貨，最慢的則是一般的郵局包裹（postal air parcel）了。

2. 快遞最快但也最貴，從運費支付方來看，可分賣方付（freight prepaid）與買方付（freight collect）兩種。而就算是已在很快的快遞類裡，還是可再細分速度的不同等級，如優先處理型服務（priority service）或一般經濟型服務（economy service）。

3. 出貨要有保障，可從兩方面使力，一個是貨品要有保險（insurance）了，另一個就是貨出了門還能追蹤得了（trackable）！

✉ 字彙 應用搶先看：E-mail 會這麼寫！

1. You can choose from express, sea and air freight for shipping your order depending on your budget and when you need your order to arrive.

您訂單的出貨方式有快遞、海運、空運可選擇，就看您的預算，以及您要您的訂單何時到貨了。

2. We offer the following shipping methods:

- Airmail: Uninsured and untrackable, between 5-7 days delivery to Europe, longer to other parts of the world.

- UPS (various services): insured and trackable – delivery speed can be next day for some parts of the world if the proper service is chosen.

我們有提供下列的出貨方式：

一郵寄：沒有保險，無法追蹤，寄到歐洲約 5～7 天可到貨，寄到其他區域則需時更長些。

一UPS（多種服務）：有保險，可追蹤，若選擇適當的服務類型，有些區域可在隔天就到貨。

字彙 應用開口說：電話要這麼講！ Track 47

D ▶ Distributor 代理商　　**M** ▶ Manufacturer 廠商

D ▶ Hi, I'm calling to follow up on the order that I sent you yesterday.

代理商 ▶ 嗨，我打來是要問一下有關我們昨天所發訂單的後續狀況。

M ▶ Yeah, I'm currently working on it! I just found that you didn't mention your preferred shipping method on the order.

廠商 ▶ 好的，我現在就正在處理您這張訂單呢！我剛剛發現您在訂單上並沒有提到您想要什麼樣的出貨方式。

D ▶ Oh! Sorry for missing that info! Please ship it to us by FedEx international priority express. It'll take just 3 days to be delivered to us.

代理商 ▶ 喔！抱歉漏了這個資訊！請幫我們安排走 FedEx 國際優先型快遞出貨，這樣只要 3 天我們就會收到貨。

M ▶ Okay, do you want to use our FedEx account for this shipment or yours?

廠商 ▶ 好的，您要我們用您的 FedEx 帳戶出貨，還是用我們的呢？

D ▶ Please use ours.

代理商 ▶ 請走我們的FedEx 帳戶出貨。

M ▶ Got it! If so, we'll charge you only $80 for the box and dry ice fee.

廠商 ▶ 收到！若是這樣，那我們就只會另外跟您收取 $80 的箱子與乾冰費用。

D ▶ No problem! Thanks!

代理商 ▶ 沒問題！謝謝！

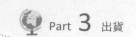
字字 計較說分明

 Track 48

coordinate [ko`ɔrdnɪt]　*v.*　協調、調節

例 We plan to coordinate a short distributor meetup at our booth for the coming conference.

在即將舉辦的會議中，我們打算在我們的攤位上協調安排個短短的代理商會面時間。

---

courier [`kʊrɪɚ]　*n.*　快遞公司、快遞員

例 We ship all products through FedEx International Priority unless the customer has their own courier.

我們所有產品都是走 FedEx 國際優先型的方式出貨，除非客戶有自己配合的快遞公司。

---

economy [ɪ`kɑnəmɪ]　*n.*　節約、經濟

例 If you need me to solicit a FedEx International Economy Air or Sea Freight quote for you, please just let me know.

若是您要我向聯邦快遞要求報來國際經濟型空運或海運的運費，就請告訴我。

相關字 economic [ˌikə`nɑmɪk]　*adj.*　經濟上的、合算的；
economical [ˌikə`nɑmɪkl̩]　*adj.*　經濟實惠的、節約的

---

express [ɪk`sprɛs]　*n.*　快遞；　*v.*　表達、陳述

例 The order will be shipped via Federal Express P1 International Service by next Wednesday.

這筆訂單將會在下星期三前，以聯邦快遞 P1 國際服務型的方式出貨。

---

forwarder [`fɔrwədə]　*n.*　運輸業者、運送者

例 If you choose a freight forwarder option, please note that you will be responsible for coordinating all paperwork and scheduling the pick-up. 若是你選擇透過貨物承攬業務代理公司（簡稱貨代）辦理出貨，請注意您就必須負責安排所有的文書作業與取貨事宜。

---

priority [praɪ`ɔrətɪ]　*n.*　優先、優先事項

例 Please rest assured that the quality is always our first priority. We'll make sure that the product quality will not be affected during transport.

請放心，品質一向是我們的首要堅持，我們會確定產品品質在運送途中不會受到影響。

3-2 包裝 Packaging

Please have it packed with...

字彙 導覽解說

1. **包裝材質百百種**：貨品打包裝箱從裡到外都有不同的包裝材質（Packing / Packaging materials），像是在袋裡或箱裡為了避免貨品晃動而放置的填充物（fillers），如泡泡粒（loose fill peanuts），到包裝外層的容器（container），如紙板箱（carton）、保麗龍箱子（Expanded polystyrene〔EPS〕box）等等。

2. **產品特殊，包裝不比尋常**：有些貨品需要特殊包裝，以避免在運送途中因環境因素而影響了品質，以對光線敏感（light sensitive）的產品來說，原廠就可能會以褐色玻璃瓶（amber glass vial）來裝瓶，若對溫度敏感（temperature sensitive），出貨時就會配上冷卻劑（refrigerant）或乾冰（dry ice）來出貨。

3. **多重多大**：包裝後的貨品有多重多大就跟運費有關了，所以客戶就會想知道貨品的毛重（gross weight）與尺寸大小（size、dimensions）這些資訊，好來估算一下運費。

字彙 應用搶先看：E-mail 會這麼寫！

1. Please send the product back in the original box (or any similar insulate box). The product is temperature sensitive and must be shipped at the appropriate temperature. So please have it packed with frozen gels and a minimum of 30lbs dry ice.

   請以原出貨箱子（或任何類似的絕緣箱）將此產品退回給我們，因為此產品對溫度敏感，必須在適合的溫度下退回，因此，請與冷凍凝膠一起包裝，同時箱內至少要放 30 磅的乾冰。

2. We put as many ice packs as we can in the EPS box. Please note that these items are perishable and must be temperature controlled. Any delay in customs could damage the product.

   我們在保麗龍箱子裡盡可能地多放冰包，請注意這些產品易腐壞，必須有溫度控制，若通關有任何延遲發生，都會損壞產品。

字彙 應用開口說：電話要這麼講！ ◎ Track 50

M ▶ Manufacturer 廠商　　**D** ▶ Distributor 代理商

M ▶ Hi, I'm happy to inform you that the new catalogs have been released!

廠商 ▶ 嗨，很高興要來告訴你新型錄已印出來了囉！

D ▶ That's great! I was just wondering if your new catalogs could be sent in time for our exhibition next Friday!

代理商 ▶ 太棒了！我剛才還在想你們的新型錄來不來得及供我們下星期五的展覽用呢！

M ▶ I do know you need them urgently! I'm calling to check how many catalogs you'd like.

廠商 ▶ 我知道你急著要呢！我打來就是要問問你要多少本型錄。

D ▶ Please tell me first how many catalogs will be packed in one carton and what its gross weight and dimensions are. I need the information to decide the exact quantity we need.

代理商 ▶ 請先告訴我一下一箱可裝幾本，還有一箱的毛重跟尺寸有多少。我需要這些資訊來決定我們要的量。

M ▶ Okay! I just happened to have those figures on hand! There'll be 50 copies in one carton. The dimensions of each box are 17" x 11" x 3" and the gross weight is 22lbs.

廠商 ▶ 好的！我剛好手邊有這些數字！每一個紙板箱的尺寸為 17" x 11" x 3"，毛重有 22磅。

D ▶ Got it! So... we'd like to have 200 catalogs, which will be 4 cartons.

代理商 ▶ 瞭解！那麼……，我們想要 200 份型錄，也就是 4 箱。

M ▶ No problem! I'll send them out to you by this Friday!

廠商 ▶ 沒問題！我會在這個星期五之前寄出給你！

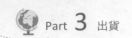

 Track 51

字字 計較說分明

container [kən`tenɚ] *n.* 容器（如箱、盒等）、貨櫃

例 Please note that you must keep the container tightly closed when storing.

儲存時請注意要將容器緊緊關好。

相關字 contain *[kən`ten]* *v.* 裝有、容納

搭配詞 sealed container 密封容器

Full-Container-Loads (FCL) shipping 整櫃運送；

Less-Than-Container Loads (LCL) Shipping 併櫃運送

---

dimension [dɪ`mɛnʃən] *n.* 尺寸、大小

例 We don't know exactly how much the freight is because the rate is calculated based on dimension and weight.

我們還不知道確切的運費是多少，因為費率要用尺寸大小和重量來算。

---

gross [gros] *adj.* 總的

例 The roughly estimated gross weight of this box is 50~60 lbs.

這箱子的毛重估算起來差不多有 50～60 磅。

packaging [`pækɪdʒɪŋ] *n.* 包裝、包裝材料

例 Proper packaging can help ensure that your goods arrive safely.

合適的包裝有助於確保您的貨品可安全抵達。

sensitive [`sɛnsətɪv] *adj.* 敏感的

例 The product material is light sensitive and should therefore be protected from direct sunlight and UV sources.

這項產品對光線敏感,因此應避免直接日曬及紫外線光源。

temperature [`tɛmprətʃɚ] *n.* 溫度、氣溫

例 This product is temperature sensitive and therefore please make sure that the parcel is being stored at the appropriate temperature.

這項產品對溫度敏感,因此,請確認包裹有儲存在合適的溫度之下。

3-3 出貨文件
Shipping Documents

Attached please find the complete set of shipping documents...

出貨文件（shipping documents）缺一不可、不及時來不可，上頭資料有誤也不可，一定要通通到位，來貨與資料全部相符，才能闖關（海關）成功！到底出貨文件有哪些呢？我們這就來看看囉！

1. **提單**：提單是廠商出貨時所填的單據，通常是由貨運承攬業者（forwarder）提供，是兩造之間對託運貨物所立下的合約。提單有分空、海運提單，在空運提單裡又分有兩種：主提單（Master Air Waybill、Master AWB），以及分提單（House Air Waybill；House AWB），而海運提單則叫做 Bill of Lading（B/L）。

2. **商業發票**（Commercial Invoice）：商業發票是具有效力的買賣證明單據，上頭會載明該批運送貨物的規格、型號、包裝與金額等資訊。

3. **裝箱單（Packing List、Packing Slip）**：裝箱單是貨品內容的說明憑證，跟商業發票的內容大致相同，差別僅在於商業發票有列金額，而裝箱單則只管貨，不管金額。

字彙 應用搶先看：E-mail 會這麼寫！

1. Your order has been shipped earlier today and should arrive shortly. Please note the AWB no. is 610792120117. Per your request, <u>attached please find the complete set of shipping documents.</u> The original ones will be packed together with the shipment.

   您的訂單在今天稍早時已出貨，應該很快就可到貨，請注意提單號碼為 610792120117。另依您所要求，<u>我在此附上一份完整的出貨文件</u>，正本將會隨貨寄出。

2. Once your order has been processed, our dispatch team will contact you and send you the shipping documents, including Packing Slip, commercial Invoice and also the Invoice for payment.

   等處理了您的訂單之後，我們的出貨人員就會立即跟您連絡，寄送出貨文件給您，文件包括裝箱單、商業發票，以及供付款所用的發票。

字彙 應用開口說：電話要這麼講！ Track 53

D ▶ Distributor 代理商   M ▶ Manufacturer 廠商

D ▶ I've got your shipping notification and the Commercial Invoice. Could you also e-mail me the rest of shipping documents?

代理商▶ 我有收到了你發來的出貨通知跟商業發票，可不可以也請你 e-mail 其他的出貨文件給我呢？

M ▶ Not a problem! So you need the AWB and Packing Slip, right?

廠商▶ 沒問題！所以你要的還有提單跟裝箱單，對嗎？

D ▶ Correct!

代理商▶ 沒錯！

M ▶ Do you require any other data for clearing the shipment from your customs this time?

廠商▶ 那你這次還有要其他的資料供清關用嗎？

D ▶ Oh! You reminded me! Please also send me the shipped product's data sheet in

代理商▶ 喔！你倒提醒了我！請你也將出貨產品的說明書發給我，以免你們這次

case your shipment was chosen for inspection by our customs again this time.

的出貨又被海關抽到要檢查。

M ▶ Yeah! It's better for us to be ready at all times! I'll get all those documents and e-mail them to you right after our phone call.

廠商 ▶ 對呀！我們最好是隨時準備就緒呢！等我們一説完電話，我就會馬上將這些文件發給你。

D ▶ You're SO great! I know you can always manage to get what we want immediately!

代理商 ▶ 你真的是太棒了！我就知道你都能馬上給我們所要的！

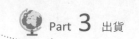
 Track 54

commercial [kə`mɝʃəl] *adj.* 商業的

例 We always declare the true value of our products on Commercial Invoices for Customs clearance.

我們在商業發票上都是列出產品的真實金額，以辦理清關。

---

lading [`ledɪŋ] *n.* 裝載

例 Please let me know what additional paperwork aside from the commercial invoice and packing list (i.e. bill of lading, Shipper's Letter of Instruction, etc.) that you require.

請告訴我除了商業發票與裝箱單之外，您還需要哪些其他的文件（如提單、出貨人的指示信函等）。

---

master [`mæstɚ] *adj.* 主要的、總的

例 A Master Air Waybill (MAWB) is issued by the carrier and not the freight forwarder.

空運主提單是由航空運輸公司出具，而不是貨代。

其他字義 *n.* 主人、大師、碩士

---

original [ə`rɪdʒənl] *adj.* 原始的、本來的；*n.* 原版、原物

例 We will send the original statement to you today via Federal Express. There will not be an additional charge as our authority agreed to waive the fee due to their overlook of the statement.

我們今天將會以 FedEx 快遞寄送正本聲明函給你，不會另外收費，因為是我們主管機關的疏忽，所以他們同意免費出具。

---

slip [slɪp]　*n.*　紙條、片條

例 Please be reminded to enclose the original Packing Slip with the shipment.

提醒您一下，請將裝箱單正本附在所出的貨裡。

其他字義　*v.*　滑動

---

waybill [`weˌbɪl]　*n.*　運貨單

例 The waybill is your express shipment's ticket and passport to ensure timely, accurate and secure delivery.

這張提單是您快遞貨物的票證與護照，以確保能及時、準確並安全地出貨。

3-4 提單 Air Waybill

Attached please find the AWB...

字彙 導覽解說

　　光看各份出貨文件的內容量，就知道提單可是最重要的「要件」，裡頭密密麻麻的欄位與小字，處處可都是進出口的必要資訊呢！我們在這兒就以空運提單為例，挑出其中的要項來瞭解一下提單囉！

1. **相關人**：Shipper's Name and Address 出貨人名稱與地址；Consignee's Name and Address 收貨人名稱與地址；Issuing Carrier's Agent Name and City 開立提單之航空運輸公司代理之名稱與所在城市。

2. **怎麼飛**：Airport of Departure and Requested Routing 出發機場與要求路線；Airport of Destination 目的地機場；Requested Flight / Date 要求之航班 / 日期。

3. **貨物事**：No. of Pieces RCP（Rate Combination Point）運價點件數；Gross Weight 毛重；Commodity Item No 貨品型號；Nature and Quantity of Goods (incl. Dimensions or Volume) 貨物品名與數量（包含尺寸或體積）。

4. **計價事**：Currency 幣別；Rate Class 運費費率等級；Rate / Charge 運費費率；Weight Charge 計費重量；Prepaid 預付 / Collect 到付；Declared Value for Carriage 運輸聲明價；Declared Value for Customs 海關聲明價；Amount of Insurance 保險金額。

字彙 應用搶先看：E-mail 會這麼寫！

1. I've asked Singapore Airlines to make an amendment to the discussed AWB. Attached please find the Amended AWB.

   我已要求新加坡航空修改我們討論的那份提單了，請見提單修改版如附。

字彙 應用開口說：電話要這麼講！ Track 56

D ▶ Distributor 代理商　**M** ▶ Manufacturer 廠商

D ▶ Hi, I need your help for the shipment sent to us yesterday.

代理商 ▶ 嗨，關於昨天你出給我們的貨，我得請你幫個忙。

M ▶ What's the matter?

廠商 ▶ 什麼事呢？

D ▶ Your shipment has arrived at our airport, but it is stuck in our customs!

代理商 ▶ 你們出的貨已經到了我們的機場，但卡在海關出不來！

M ▶ Do you need anything from us?

廠商 ▶ 有需要我們怎麼做嗎？

D ▶ Yeah! We just found that our customer applied for this product's import permit by using our mother company's name as the importer, not ours. So we need you to amend the

代理商 ▶ 有的！我們剛剛才知道我們客戶所申請的產品進口許可證，上頭的進口人寫成我們的母公司，而不是我們。因此，我們得要請你更改空運提單上的收貨人資

consignee info on the Air Waybill.

料。

M ▶ I see... I will request the airline make this amendment. But, as far as I know, an administration fee will be charged for any amendment.

廠商 ▶ 瞭解……，我會跟航空公司修改，不過，就我所知，有任何的修改都要加收行政費用喔！

D ▶ Okay, no problem. Just issue to us another Invoice for this fee. We hope to get the correct Air Waybill from you asap!

代理商 ▶ 好的，沒問題，對這個費用，就請再出具一張發票給我們。我們希望能夠盡快拿到那張正確的空運提單！

 Track 57

字字 計較說分明

carriage [`kærɪdʒ] *n.* 運輸、運費

例 Shipper may increase the limitation of liability by declaring a higher value for carriage and paying a supplemental charge if required.

出貨人可申報較高的運輸價值並支付附加費用，以擴充責任限度。

---

commodity [kə`mɑdətɪ] *n.* 商品

例 The energy commodity market is extremely volatile and driven by geopolitical factors.

能源商品的市場極為複雜多變，而且會受地緣政治因素所影響。

專有名詞 CCC Code (Standard Classification of Commodities of the Republic of China Code) 中華民國商品標準分類號列

---

consignee [ˌkɑnsaɪ`ni] *n.* 收貨人、承銷人

例 This statement may be included on the import certificate; however, if it is not, the consignee (importer) must make a certification.

這則聲明應要在進口證上列出，若沒有的話，則收貨人（進

126

口人）就必須另行出具一份證明。

---

customs [ˈkʌstəmz]　*n.*　海關

例 Please note that you are solely responsible for any customs clearance fees required.

請注意，您必須全額負擔清關所收取的任何費用。

---

declare [dɪˋklɛr]　*v.*　申報、聲明

例 The goods declared on the Air Waybill are apparently in good order and condition for carriage.

提單中所申報的貨品狀況良好，可供運送。

---

route [rut]　*v.*　安排路線；　*n.*　路線

例 The *ABA* routing number is a 9-digit identification number assigned to financial institutions by The American Bankers Association (ABA).

ABA 路徑號碼是美國銀行協會設定給金融機構的九碼辨識號碼。

3-5 通關 Customs Clearance

The customs need clearance instructions from the recipient...

字彙 導覽解說

越洋打通關的規矩多，情況也多，我們在此就以出口報關（Export customs declaration）為例，來看看它的一步步流程囉！

1. 報關人傳輸出口報單資料／Declarant transmitting export declaration data

2. 中華民國貿易及通關自動化網路 TRADE-VAN (T/V; VAN – Value Added Network)

3. 海關電腦貨物篩選系統／Cargo Selectivity System：
   （專家系統篩選出三種通關方式）
   ・C1 免審免驗（Free of Paper and Cargo）
   ・C2 文件審核（Document Scrutiny）
   ・C3 貨物查驗（Cargo Examination）

4. 分類估價計稅：Tariff classification, valuation and duty

5. 放行／Authorizing release

通關最怕卡關（get stuck at customs），當出貨文件出缺，或是所列與實物不符時，都會造成通關遲延（clearance delay），這時可就要快快處理呢！

字彙 應用搶先看：E-mail 會這麼寫！

1. This shipment needs to go through document scrutiny at our customs. Since total 3 boxes were shipped, we're requested to submit the Packing List which contains box no. on it. Please revise your Packing List accordingly and e-mail to me asap.

   這次的出貨得經過我們海關的文件審核程序，因為總共出了三箱，海關要求我們提供的裝箱單要列有箱號，還請您依照要求修改裝箱單，並請盡快 e-mail 給我。

2. We noticed that your package has encountered a clearance delay and stuck in your customs. The customs need clearance instructions from the recipient so as to authorize release.

   我們注意到出給您的包裹在通關上有延遲，卡在您們的海關，而海關需要收貨人的清關指示才能放行。

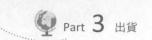
字彙 應用開口說：電話要這麼講！ Track 59

M ▶ Manufacturer 廠商　**D** ▶ Distributor 代理商

M ▶ Hi, FedEx told us that the parcel shipped last Friday is undergoing a clearance delay. Have you got any news?

廠商 ▶ 嗨，我們的FedEx 說我們上星期五出的貨現在通關有延遲，請問您知道這個消息嗎？

D ▶ Yeah! We knew about that this morning! We've contacted our local FedEx to see what is required to speed up the custom clearance.

代理商 ▶ 有的！我們今天早上知道了這件事，也有跟我們當地的 FedEx 連絡了，看是有需要提供什麼，才能快點清關。

M ▶ Do you need any documents from me?

廠商 ▶ 您有要我這兒的什麼文件嗎？

D ▶ Yes! We're requested by our customs to provide the shipped product's data sheet.

代理商 ▶ 沒錯！海關要求我們提供出貨產品的說明書。

M▶ Not a problem! I can e-mail the data sheet to you later.

廠商▶ 沒問題！我等一下就會 e-mail 說明書給您。

D▶ That's great. Thanks for your help!

代理商▶ 太好了，謝謝您的幫忙！

M▶ You're welcome! Hope the clearance issue will be resolved quickly and the package can be released soon!

廠商▶ 不用客氣，希望通關問題趕快解決，貨可以盡快放行呢！

 Track 60

classification [ˌklæsəfəˋkeʃən] *n.* 分類、分級

例 These products will have a GHS (Globally Harmonized System of Classification and Labeling of Chemicals) sticker on the inner packaging of the plastic bag.

這些產品會在塑袋內包裝上有張 GHS（化學品分類與標示之全球調和系統）標籤。

declaration [ˌdɛkləˋreʃən] *n.* （納稅品等的）申報、宣告、聲明

例 Our products do not require a DEFRA[1] Certificate for customs purposes, but please confirm if they require any other kind of declaration.

我們的產品不需要 DEFRA 證明來清關，但請跟我們確認是否海關有需要任何其他的聲明。

相關字 declare *[dɪˋklɛr]* *v.*

註[1]：DEFRA: Department for Environment, Food and Rural Affairs／英國環境、食品與鄉村事務部

duty [ˋdjutɪ] *n.* 稅、責任

例 We will waive both the freight and duty / tax charges if you can provide your own FedEx account for the shipment.

若是此次出貨您可提供您們自己的 FedEx 帳號，那我們就不會跟您收運費和稅負費用。

搭配詞 customs duty 關稅；import / export duty 進口／出口稅

---

examination [ɪgˌzæməˈneʃən] *n.* 檢查

例 In addition to the following scheduled examinations, the equipment will still require a thorough examination.

除了已排定的下列檢查項目之外，此設備還需要再進行徹底的檢查。

---

scrutiny [ˈskrutnɪ] *n* 仔細檢查

例 We have the most developed and comprehensive document scrutiny system in the European Union countries.

在歐盟國家裡，我們擁有最先進、最完整的文件檢查系統。

---

tariff [ˈtærɪf] *n.* 關稅、稅率

例 All items in this shipment are under harmonized tariff system code: 38220000.

此次出貨的所有品項都是屬於統一關稅系統編碼 38220000 項下的產品。

4-1 付款條件
Terms of Payment

If you are sending the payment using...

字彙 導覽解說

付款條件是交易裡的一大要點，它可有好幾種不同的規矩，以及不同的條件設定！我們在這兒就來列個幾種主要的付款條件，看看它們的全名與頭字語囉！

☑ 信用狀：Letter of Credit (L/C)

☑ 付款交單：Document against Payment (D/P)

☑ 承兌交單：Document against Acceptance (D/A)

☑ 憑單據付款：Cash against Documents (CAD)

☑ 貨到付款：Cash on Delivery (COD)

☑ 預付貨款：Cash in Advance (CIA)、Payment in Advance (PIA)、Cash before shipment (CBS)、Prepayment

☑ 月結：Net monthly account

☑ 發票日後 30 天付款：Net 30

☑ 貨到付款：Cash on delivery (COD)

☑ 發票日隔月的 15 日：the 15th of the month following

invoice date (15 MFI)

☑ 發票日後 10 天內付款可享 1%折扣，否則為發票日後 30 天付款 ：1% discount if payment received within 10 days, otherwise payment 30 days after invoice date (1% 10 Net 30)

✉字彙 應用搶先看：E-mail 會這麼寫！

1. For export orders, we always ask our customers to make payment in advance. But, as a gesture of goodwill, I could make an exception for you and accept "net 10 days" as an alternative way of payment.

   對於出口訂單，我們都會要求客戶預付貨款，不過，為了表示善意，我可為您破個例，接受「淨 10 天」這個不同的付款條件。

2. If you are sending the payment using Letters of Credit, please make sure that your Letter of Credit has to be irrevocable, negotiable with our bank, issued or confirmed by a first class international bank.

   若是您要用信用狀付款，請確定開不可撤銷、可讓購給我們銀行的信用狀，要由一級國際銀行來開立或保兌。

Part 4 | 付款

字彙 應用開口說：電話要這麼講！　Track 62

D ▶ Distributor 代理商　　**M** ▶ Manufacturer 廠商

D ▶ Have you got the payment that we wired for our new order?

代理商 ▶ 請問你有收到我們新訂單的電匯貨款嗎？

M ▶ Yes, we have already received the payment and the shipment is going to be picked up by TNT today.

廠商 ▶ 有的，我們已經收到貨款了，事實上，TNT 今天就會來取走這批出貨呢！

D ▶ That's good. Taking this opportunity, I'd like to discuss with you about the terms of payment.

代理商 ▶ 那就好。藉這個機會，我想要跟你討論一下付款條件的事。

M ▶ I'm listening!

廠商 ▶ 請說！

D ▶ We'd like to know if it's possible to change our payment terms to Net 30 days instead of prepayment.

代理商 ▶ 我們想知道有沒有可能將付款條件從目前的預付貨款改成淨 30 天呢？

M ▶ It's our policy to ask our customers to make the entire payment in advance.

廠商 ▶ 我們公司的政策都是要客戶在出貨前完成預付的。

D ▶ We know that, but in fact prepayment doesn't suit us anymore because the number of our orders is increasing!

代理商 ▶ 我們也知道，不過，事實上因為我們的訂單量增加了，預付已經不合我們的情況了耶！

M ▶ That's true... Okay! We do appreciate your hard work in promoting our products. So for your company, we'll accept your proposed payment terms.

廠商 ▶ 這倒也是……，好吧！很謝謝你們努力地推廣我們公司的產品，所以，對你們公司，我們可依您所提議的付款條件來辦理。

D ▶ Great! Thanks!

代理商 ▶ 太棒了！謝謝！

Part 4 付款

 Track 63

字字計較說分明

acceptance [ək`sɛptəns] *n.* （票據等的）承兌、認付、接受

例 Documents Against Payment and Documents Against Acceptance both rely on an instrument widely used in international trade, i.e. a bill of exchange or draft.

付款交單和承兌交單都會用到國貿上常用的工具，也就是匯票。

---

against [ə`gɛnst] *prep.* 對比、對照

例 We use cash against documents as a payment term for orders between €30,000 and €100,000.

對於金額介於 30,000 到 100,000 歐元之間的訂單，我們所採用的付款條件為憑單據付款。

其他字義 反對、對抗、不利於

---

alternative [ɔl`tɝnətɪv] *adj.* 供選擇的； *n.* 二擇一、替代選項

例 If you wish to arrange alternative terms of payment, please let us know upon placing your order.

若您想要選擇另一種付款條件的話，就請您在下單時告訴我們。

---

confirm [kən`fɝm]　*v.*　確認、確定

例 An exporter with a confirmed letter of credit will be paid by the confirming bank even if the foreign buyer or the foreign bank defaults.

出口方若有保兌信用狀，即使外國買方或外國銀行不付款，保兌銀行仍須支付。

irrevocable [ɪ`rɛvəkəb!]　*adj.*　不可撤銷的

例 The terms of payment we accept are prepayment and irrevocable Letter of Credit at sight.

我們可接受的付款條件為預付與不可撤銷的即期信用狀。

相關字 revocable [`rɛvəkəb!]　*adj.*　可撤回的

revoke [rɪ`vok]　*v.*　撤回、取消

negotiable [nɪ`goʃɪəb!]　*adj.*　可轉讓的

例 Do you know negotiable documents can be exchanged for money?

你知道可轉讓的票據文件是可以兌現的嗎？

其他字義 可談判的、可商量的

Part 4 付款

4-2 付款方式
Payment Method

We accept... as payment methods.

　　除了與單據有關的付款條件之外，要將貨款付給廠商，要將錢送達對方帳戶，大多會採用這三種方式：

1. 匯款（**wire transfer**、remittance）：廠商通知匯款明細時，會提到銀行名、戶名或受益人（Account name or Beneficiary）、帳號（Account No.）、ABA Routing no.（ABA 路徑號碼）、銀行國際代碼（Swift Code），另外也多會要求銀行手續費（bank fee）須由匯款方負擔。

2. 信用卡（**credit card**）：廠商會要求付款人提出信用卡明細，包括信用卡卡別（Card type）、卡號（Card no.）、持卡人姓名（Card holder's name）、效期（Expiration date、Valid date、Good through）、三碼安全碼（3-digit security code），有的廠商還需信用卡帳單地址（Card address）的資料。而對於信用卡的交易（transaction），有的廠商得收

取處理費（processing fee）。

3. 支票（check or cheque）：廠商會通知付款人支票寄送的地址，收件人多會要求寫為「應收帳款」（Accounts Receivable）部門。

✉ 字彙 應用搶先看：E-mail 會這麼寫！

1. <u>We accept checks, credit cards, and wire transfers as payment methods.</u> However, a $50 fee applies to all invoices paid via wire transfer due to high bank fees on our end.

   <u>我們可接受以支票、信用卡及匯款付款的方式，</u>不過，若以匯款支付，因我們這邊銀行所收的銀行手續費高，故所有發票貨款須再加上$50。

2. For credit card transactions, we'll surcharge additional 3% as processing fee. Also please fill out the attached credit card authorization form and send it back to us.

   我們對信用卡交易會另收 3%的處理費，另也請填寫所附的信用卡授權書，填完後再發回給我們。

Part 4 ｜付款

 **字彙** 應用開口說：電話要這麼講！ Track 65

M ▶ Manufacturer 廠商　　**D** ▶ Distributor 代理商

M ▶ I just got your e-mail informing us of your credit card details. Unfortunately, due to security issues, we are not able to accept or process credit card transactions via email!

廠商 ▶ 我剛剛收到妳的 e-mail，通知我們信用卡明細，不過，因為安全因素，我們無法透過e-mail 來接受或處理信用卡交易耶！

D ▶ I see! So... could I just give you the card details again on the phone right now?

代理商 ▶ 瞭解！所以……，請問我可以現在就在電話上給妳信用卡明細嗎？

M ▶ Yes, please!.

廠商 ▶ 可以的，請說！

D ▶ Okay, here is our card information... Our Visa card no. is 4365 1202 0925 1220 and it's good through May 2021.

代理商 ▶ 好的，我這就給妳我們的信用卡資料……，Visa 卡卡號是4365 1202 0925 1220，效期是到 2021年五月。

M ▶ Got it! I also need the 3-digit security code on the back of the card.

廠商 ▶ 收到！我還需要卡片背後所列的三碼安全碼。

D ▶ Right! It's 936.

代理商 ▶ 對對對！安全碼是936。

M ▶ Okay... It's done! Thanks for your help and also your understanding of our security policy on credit card payments.

廠商 ▶ 好的……，扣款完成！謝謝妳的幫忙，也謝謝妳體諒配合我們信用卡付款的安全政策。

Part 4 ｜付款

Track 66

account [ə`kaʊnt]　*n.*　帳戶、帳目、客戶

例 We will not be able to fulfill any further purchase orders while these accounts remain unpaid, and reserve the right to add interest on to late payments.

在這些帳款尚未付清前,我們將無法執行任何訂單,而對於遲付貨款,我們也保有收取利息的權利。

---

digit [`dɪdʒɪt]　*n.*　數字

例 Could we please have the 3-digit security code for the credit card you are using for payment?

能否請您告知您用來付款的那張信用卡的三碼安全碼?

---

payable [`peəbḷ]　*adj.*　應支付的

例 If you have any queries regarding your invoices, please call the Accounts Payable Helpline.

若是您對您的發票有任何問題,請撥打我們的應付帳款諮詢專線。

---

receivable [rɪˋsivəbl̩]　*adj.*　應收的　*n.*　應收帳款

例 Please contact our Account Receivable Department for new bank accounts information.

請跟我們的應收帳款部門聯絡，問問新銀行帳戶的資料。

remittance [rɪˋmɪtns]　*n.*　匯款、匯款額

例 As of the 18th of January 2017, our BANK Account details have changed. Please make sure to send your remittance to the correct account.

我們銀行帳戶資料自 2017 年 1 月 18 日起已更改，請您確認您的匯款會匯至正確的帳戶。

SWIFT [swɪft] 頭字語：Society for Worldwide Interbank Financial Telecommunication 全球銀行金融電訊協會

例 We just wired the payment to your account but our bank said the given SWIFT code for your bank is incorrect. Please reply asap enabling us to complete the payment.

我們剛匯款到您的帳戶，但銀行說您們所給的銀行國際代碼不正確，請盡快回覆，好讓我們能完成付款。

其他字義　*adj.*　快速的、快捷的

Part 4 付款

4-3 信用狀 Letter of Credit

We can accept Letter of Credit at sight...

 Track 67

　　信用狀是將國際交易多拉了銀行這一個保證人進來，所以可確保交易更為妥當，可降低買方不買帳的風險，也讓廠商出貨能夠出得安心！我們這就來看看這份加持了安心的信用狀裡有什麼要點囉！

1. **各方人馬**：買方為信用狀的申請人（Applicant），賣方為受益人（Beneficiary）；開狀銀行（Issuing Bank）開立信用狀後，會寄發給通知銀行（Advising Bank）；付款者為付款行（Drawee）。

2. **檢查要點**：信用狀上所列的項目都要與合約相符，所以要點、細節都得逐一細看囉：

   1) **金錢事**：幣別（Currency）、金額（Amount）、金額上下寬容百分比（Tolerance）

   2) **匯票事**：匯票種類可分－憑即期匯票付款（Available by

drafts at sight）、開立□天的期票（Draft(s) to be drawn at... days）、遠期匯票（Time drafts）

3) **產品事**：貨品／服務內容（Description of Goods / Service）

4) **文件事**：所需文件（Documents Required）包括有已簽署之商業發票（Commercial Invoice）、海運提單或空運提單（Bill of Lading or Air Waybill）、保險單據（Insurance Policy or Certificate）、裝箱單（Packing List）等。

5) **出貨事**：接管地／發送地（Place of Taking in Charge / Dispatch From）、裝載港／起運機場（Port of Loading / Airport of Departure）、卸貨港／目的地機場（Port of Discharge / Airport of Destination）、最終目的地（Place of Final Destination）、最後裝運日期（Latest Date of Shipment）、可否分批出貨（Partial Shipment Permitted / Allowed or Prohibited）與轉運（Transhipment）

6) **付款事**：要求須從運送日次日起□天內提出單據以押匯（Documents to be Presented for Negotiation within □ Days after Date of Shipment），以及寫明所有銀行費用由申請人或受益人負擔（All Banking Charges are for Applicant's or Beneficiary's Account）。

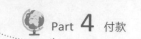 **字彙** 應用開口說：電話要這麼講！ Track 68

M ▶ Manufacturer 廠商　C ▶ Customer 客戶

M ▶ For orders to overseas destinations, we can only accept Letters of Credit at sight.

廠商 ▶ 對於出到海外的訂單，我們只能接受即期信用狀。

C ▶ Hmm... We've never issued a Letter of Credit before...

客戶 ▶ 嗯……，我們還從來沒開過信用狀……。

M ▶ Don't worry! It's not so complicated. You just need to fill out and complete an application requesting your bank to issue an L / C in favor of our company.

廠商 ▶ 不要擔心！不會太複雜，您只要填寫個申請表，要求您的銀行開立信用狀給我們公司就可以了。

C ▶ So what should be written on an L / C application?

客戶 ▶ 那申請表會要填寫些什麼呢？

M ▶ Just remember that all data needs to correspond to the

廠商 ▶ 只要記著上頭所寫的每一點都要符合我們買賣合

terms and conditions in our purchase and sales agreement.

約上的條件就可以了。

C▶ Okay. That sounds easy! If we need your help and advice when issuing the L / C, we'll ask you!

客戶▶ 好的，聽起來還容易！要是我們開信用狀時有需要什麼協助跟建議，我們就會來請教您！

M▶ Yeah! If you have any other questions, please feel free to ask me anytime!

廠商▶ 是啊！如果您有其他的問題，就請隨時問我囉！

Part 4 付款

字字 計較說分明

draft [dræft]　*n.*　匯票、匯款單

例 An international bank draft is a secure way to send money to someone in another country.

國際銀行的匯票是寄錢給其他國家的人的一種安全的方式。

其他字義　*n.*　草稿；　*v.*　起草、設計

---

drawee [drɔ`i]　*n.*　付款人

例 The drawee is generally the importer or the collecting bank.

付款人通常是進口人或是代收銀行。

---

issue [`ɪʃʊ]　*v.*　出具、開立、發行

例 We can issue a Letter of Credit so as to provide a secure means of payment to your overseas suppliers.

我們可以開立信用狀，給您的海外供應商提供個安全的付款方式。

---

permit [pɚ`mɪt]　*v.*　允許、准許

例 Partial shipments shall be permitted unless otherwise agreed.

除非另有協議，否則是允許分批出貨的。

其他字義 *[`pɜ·mɪt]*   *n.*   許可證、執照

---

prohibit [prə`hɪbɪt]   *v.*   （以法令、規定等）禁止

例 Problems may arise if transhipment is prohibited, as transport is a complex business these days.

若是禁止轉運，可能會有問題發生，因為現今的運輸複雜多了。

---

tolerance [`tɑlərəns]   *n.*   容許偏差、誤差

例 The Supplier shall be deemed to have fulfilled its contract if the goods delivered fell within this tolerance of plus or minus five percent (5%) of the quantity ordered.

若所出貨品的數量誤差值在所訂數量的上下 5%以內的話，那將視此供應商已履行了合約。

其他字義   *n.*   寬容、忍耐

Part 4 付款

4-4 催款 Payment Collection

Our records indicate the attached invoice is past **due**.

字彙 導覽解說

　　不管你買貨後的付款動作是不是一向很準時，一樣都會經常收到廠商發來催款信，因為廠商在買方付款日還沒到時可來個付款提醒，一到了到期日還沒收到貨款，當然也就可以名正言順地大催特催了。發票逾期怎説？催款怎催？我們現就來説説、催催囉！

1. **逾期怎說**：發票上都有個付款到期日（due date），過了這日期就犯了逾期（past due、overdue）、未付（outstanding、unpaid）的失誤了！

2. **催款怎催**：催錢都有些固定的説法，大多會是請你就快快安排付款（arrange payment、make payment、settle accounts），若廠商覺得雲淡風輕地説不夠力，就會祭出禁令與罰則，跟你説個明白：

   1) 往後訂單暫停受理（unable to fulfill any further purchase orders）

2) 利息要算（apply interest on late payments）

3) 追帳成本要收（recover the costs of debt collection）

📧 字彙 應用搶先看：E-mail 會這麼寫！

1. Our records indicate the attached invoice is past due. Please acknowledge receipt of this email immediately and arrange for prompt payment of this overdue amount.

我們的紀錄顯示附件的發票已逾期了，請立即回覆您有收到此 email，也請盡速支付此逾期貨款金額。

2. Please settle all the accounts immediately as they are substantially overdue. Please acknowledge receipt of this notice and indicate the date that the payment will be made. Please be reminded that Interest will be payable on all accounts due and outstanding for over 30 days at the rate of 2% per month from the due date of invoice to the date of payment.

請立即付清所有款項，因已逾期多時，請您回覆有收到此通知，並告知將於哪一天付款。在此提醒您，所有逾期 30 天仍未付的貨款將以月息 2 厘計算利息，所計期間由發票到期日起，計至付款日為止。

Part 4 付款

153

字彙 應用開口說：電話要這麼講！ Track 71

M ▶ Manufacturer 廠商　　**D** ▶ Distributor 代理商

M ▶ Hi, I just got your new order, but I'd like to remind you that your Invoice # 925 is still overdue!

廠商 ▶ 嗨，我剛收到你的新訂單，不過我要提醒你一下，你們發票號碼 925 的這一張發票還逾期未付喔！

D ▶ Really? I'm not aware that we still have any outstanding invoices! I'll check with our Accounting Department!

代理商 ▶ 真的嗎？我不知道我們還有任何未付款的發票！我會跟我們的會計部門查查。

M ▶ Please help and do so right away. You know that we are unable to accept any new purchase orders while the account remains unpaid.

廠商 ▶ 還請你馬上協助處理，你知道若還有未清帳款，我們是不能處理任何後續訂單的。

D ▶ Yes, I know your company policy.

代理商 ▶ 是的，我知道你們公司的這個政策。

M▶ If necessary, I could e-mail the overdue Invoice to your Accounting Department. By the way, please also provide the direct contact details of the administrator with responsibility for our account.

廠商▶ 如果有必要的話，我可以 e-mail 這張逾期發票給你們的會計部門。對了，也請告訴我負責我們帳務那位管理人員的聯絡明細。

D▶ Sure! I'll send my coworker's information to you and I'll also ask her to make contact with you directly!

代理商▶ 沒問題！我會給你我同事的資料，也會請她直接跟你連絡喔！

M▶ Great! Thanks!

廠商▶ 太好了！謝謝你！

 Track 72

debt [dɛt]　*n.*　債、借款、負債

例 We'll charge late payment interest to help recover the cost of debt collection.

我們會對遲繳的貨款收取利息，以彌補催收欠款所產生的成本。

due [dju]　*adj.*　應支付的、到期的；　*n.*　應付款

例 Please ensure that all of these invoices have been received by yourselves and when due, they are to be paid in line with our agreed payment terms.

請確定您們都有收到這些發票了，也請確保待這些發票到期時，您們會依我們所議定的付款條件來支付貨款。

outstanding [`aʊt`stændɪŋ]　*adj.*　未償付的；　*n.*　未清帳款

例 Our records show an outstanding balance for your Order 105234. Please check and let us know when we can expect the payment.

我們的紀錄顯示您單號 105234 的這份訂單仍有餘額未清，請查一查，並告知我們何時可收到貨款。

其他字義　*adj.*　顯著的、傑出的

overdue [`ovɚ`dju] *adj.* 過期的、逾期未付的

例 Please see attached to this e-mail a copy of our invoice # SI1202 which remains outstanding and overdue for payment.

請見此 e-mail 所附的號碼 SI1202 這一張發票，它已逾期，尚未付款。

---

remain [rɪ`men] *v.* 仍是、保持、剩下、留待

例 If accounts remain unpaid, we reserve the right to add interest on late payments.

若是仍不結清帳款，我們將有權對遲繳的貨款加計利息。

---

settle [`sɛtl̩] *v.* 支付、結算、安排、解決（問題等）

例 All accounts are to be settled within 30 days from the date of invoice.

所有帳款應於發票日起 30 日內付清。

相關字 settlement [`sɛtl̩mənt] *n.*

Part 4 │ 付款

4-5 對帳單
Account Statement

I have attached a **statement** of your account.

　　買方會在幾種情況下收到廠商發來的對帳單（Statement），一是廠商定期發送，一是在有逾期未收帳款時，還有一種不是來催款，而是廠商的會計師或稽核人員（auditors）來確認未收帳款的金額。收到對帳單後會要怎麼處理呢？我們這就來看看幾個不同情況的應對囉！

1. **有沒有漏啊**：看到對帳單所列的發票清單，負責的人一定要練到不由自主地一一查查，看有無什麼發票是廠商有列，但其實並未收過的（missing any invoices）。

2. **快要到期囉**：這是定期發送對帳單的最主要目的，廠商會請買方方便時就盡快付款囉（remit payment at your earliest convenience）！

3. **逾期了**：這就是我們前一個單元所說的情況，對於逾期發票（outstanding invoices），廠商當然是發來對帳單要求買方

速速付款。若是你已付款了，但廠商還將該帳目列在帳上，就請提供銀行的匯款通知單（Remittance Advice），請廠商更新紀錄囉！

4. **查帳**：收到這類對帳單時別急著付款，你要做的動作就是泡杯咖啡，好好對一下廠商所列結算日期的應收未收餘額（balances）是否正確囉！

✉ 字彙 應用搶先看：E-mail 會這麼寫！

1. I have attached a statement of your account as of today. Please check your records to make sure that you are not missing any Invoices / Credit Memos.
   我在此附上您公司到今天的對帳單，請查查您的紀錄，確認一下是否沒有漏失所列的任何發票／貸項通知單。

2. Our auditors are auditing our financial statement and wish to obtain direct confirmation of amount shown below as of Dec. 31, 2016. Please compare with your records and note the details of differences, if any.
   我們的稽核人員正在稽核財務對帳單，希望可取得您的直接回覆，確認下面列至 2016 年 12 月 31 日的金額，請與您的紀錄比較，並標記出任何有差異的明細資料。

字彙 應用開口說：電話要這麼講！　Track 74

M ▶ Manufacturer 廠商　D ▶ Distributor 代理商

M ▶ I'm calling to check one issue with you. Did you receive the statement that our auditors sent you early this month?

廠商 ▶ 我打來是要跟您問一件事，您有收到這個月初我們稽核人員寄給您的對帳單嗎？

D ▶ Yes! I'm sorry for not yet replying to your auditors! Our Accounting Department has reviewed the statement and just gave me the checking results.

代理商 ▶ 有的！抱歉還沒回給您的稽核人員！我們的會計部門已查過了這份對帳單，也剛告訴我查核的結果了。

M ▶ Okay. So are there any differences compared to your records?

廠商 ▶ 好的，那請問跟您的紀錄資料對照後有發現什麼不同的地方嗎？

D ▶ No. The shown balance as of Dec. 31, 2016, is correct.

代理商 ▶ 沒有，所列2016年 12 月 31 日的餘額是正確的。

M ▶ That's good. So please kindly help to sign the original and return it to our auditors directly.

廠商 ▶ 那就好，請您幫忙在正本上簽名，然後直接寄回給我們的稽核人員。

D ▶ No problem. I'll ask our Accounting Manager to sign and then send it out today!

代理商 ▶ 沒問題，我會請我們的會計經理簽名，並在今天將資料寄出。

M ▶ Thanks for your cooperation!

廠商 ▶ 非常謝謝您的幫忙！

Part 4 | 付款

字字 計較說分明

 Track 75

audit [`ɔdɪt] *v.* *n.* 稽核、查帳

例 As part of our audit procedures, we would like to confirm the accounts receivable balances as of December 31, 2016.

我們稽核的程序之一是要確認 2016 年 12 月 31 日的應收帳款餘額。

---

balance [`bæləns] *n.* 結餘、平衡、均衡

例 This is not a request for payment but for audit purposes only. Payment received after June 30, 2016 is not reflected in the balance shown.

此對帳單並不是要來催收帳款,只是為了稽核之用。您在 2016 年 6 月 30 日後所付的款項並不會反映在結餘裡。

Credit Memo [`krɛdɪt `mɛmo] *n.* 貸項通知單

例 A Credit Memo is an accounting method of reducing or canceling an invoice.

貸項通知單是會計上的一個方法,用來減少發票金額或取消發票。

比較 Debit Memo *n.* 借項通知單

financial [faɪ`nænʃəl]　*adj.*　財務的、金融的

例 Our 3% price increase as well as a 10% increase in the number of sales has brought us back to financial equilibrium.

我們價格調整了 3%，再加上銷售額增加了 10%，才又將我們回復到財務平衡的狀態。

Remittance Advice [rɪ`mɪtns əd`vaɪs]　*n.*　匯款通知單

例 Please make payment within 30 days from the invoice date and notify us with a Remittance Advice once payment has been made.

請在發票日後 30 天付款，付款後也請告訴我們，發匯款通知單給我們。

---

statement [`stetmənt]　*n.*　對帳單、聲明函

例 Your statement is attached. You have exceeded your credit limit. Please remit payment at your earliest convenience, so future shipments will not be delayed.

在此附上您的對帳單，您的帳上金額已超出信用額度，還請您盡早付款，這樣之後的出貨才不會受到延誤。

Part 4 付款

5-1 索取產品資料
Requesting Product Info

I've attached the **manual** for your review.

字彙 導覽解說

　　要評估產品合不合用，好好研讀產品的相關資料就是件很重要的工作了！有研究有安心，沒研究就有可能造成後續一大串的使用問題！產品類別五花八門，產品資料的種類也就各有各的專業與精彩！我們在這兒列出些常見的產品資料，一起聞香一下囉！

1. **基本型資料**：型錄（catalog、brochure）、單張型錄（flyer、leaflet）、產品小冊（booklet）、手冊（manual）、產品資料表（Data Sheet）、規格書（Specification）、產品說明書／仿單（Package Insert）

2. **技術型資料**：操作手冊（Operating Manual）、分析報告（Certificate of Analysis）、物質安全資料表（Material Safety Data Sheet）、技術報告（Technical Report）、品管檢驗報告（QC Report）、協定（Protocol）、文獻（Reference、Literature）

3. **資料要做何用**：資料要來了之後，就該是挑燈認真研讀（study、perusal）時，要用來參考（reference）、評估（evaluation）、審視（review），也會用來跟其他產品做個比較（comparison）呢！

📧 字彙 應用搶先看：E-mail 會這麼寫！

1. I have included an updated copy of our product list with the new products added in August 2016. Additionally, I have attached two of our most recent flyers. Feel free to browse all our flyers at our website.

我有附上了我們產品表的更新版本，裡頭有 2016 年八月新增的產品。另外，附件還有我們兩份最新的單張型錄，也請上我們的網站，裡頭收有所有的單張型錄供您瀏覽。

2. I've attached the manual for your review. Also below is a link to the Certificate of Analysis for our latest lot. Please note that the actual lot received may be different depending on lot availability at the time of order placement.

我在此附上產品手冊供您詳閱，也貼上我們最新批次的分析報告連結，請注意您實際收到的貨品批次可能會有所不同，因會視您下單當時的現貨批次來決定。

 **字彙** 應用開口說：電話要這麼講！ Track 77

C ▶ Customer 客戶　M ▶ Manufacturer 廠商

C ▶ Hi, I noted from your website that you've launched a newer version of PA0926.

客戶▶ 嗨，我有看到您們的網站上說您們有推出新版的PA0926。

M ▶ Correct! The newer version utilizes the latest technology and has considerably higher nutritional contents than the older version.

廠商▶ 沒錯！新版產品使用了最新的技術，因此，它的營養成份比舊版產品高出許多。

C ▶ Could you provide your quote and its Package Insert for my evaluation?

客戶▶ 您可不可以給我報價單跟產品的仿單讓我評估一下呢？

M ▶ Sure! I'll e-mail them to you! I'll also send along other related data for your reference!

廠商▶ 當然可以！我會發e-mail 給您，也會再寄一些其他資料讓您參考囉！

Part 5 客服與客訴

C ▶ Great! By the way, do you have the data showing the comparison between the old version and new version?

客戶 ▶ 太好了！對了，請問您有新舊版產品的比較資料嗎？

M ▶ Yeah! I can send you a comparison chart for you to get a clearer picture of the differences.

廠商 ▶ 有的！我可以寄給您一份比較表，這樣您就可以更清楚看到它們之間的差別在哪裡了。

C ▶ Excellent! Thanks!

客戶 ▶ 太棒了！謝謝您！

 字字 計較說分明 Track 78

brochure [bro`ʃʊr] *n.* 型錄、小冊子

例 I would like to announce several updates regarding our brochures. They're added on our marketing material webpage and available for distribution.

在此我要宣布一下我們有推出了幾份新型錄，這些型錄也已加進網頁的行銷素材資料裡，可讓您發送給客戶。

comparison [kəm`pærəsn] *n.* 比較

例 It can be difficult for us to make comparisons between similar products which do not come in standard sizes.

我們很難在非標準規格的相似產品之間做比較。

flyer [`flaɪɚ] *n.* 單張型錄、（廣告）傳單

例 I've attached our recommended flyers for your review and use at the upcoming conference.

在此附上我們建議的單張型錄讓您看看，也讓您在即將到來的會議上使用。

insert [`ɪnsɝt]　*n.*　仿單、插入物

例 Please see the package insert for the complete list of indications, warnings, precautions, adverse events, clinical results, and other important medical information.

請看仿單資料，裡頭有列出所有的成份、警告、注意事項、副作用、臨床結果，以及其他重要的醫藥資訊。

其他字義 *[ɪn`sɝt]*　*v.*　插入

literature [`lɪtərətʃɚ]　*n.*　印刷品、文宣、文獻

例 Please remember to send all your marketing material requests through our internal literature page and fill out the form completely.

請記得透過我們內部的文宣網頁來提出您要求的行銷素材，並完整填寫申請表格。

manual [`mænjʊəl]　*n.*　手冊

例 To ensure the best performance, please read the Operating Manual before using the instrument.

為了確保有最佳的品質表現，請在使用此儀器前先閱讀這份操作手冊。

其他字義　*adj.*　手工的、手動的

5-2 索取樣品
Requesting Samples

Free samples are available upon request...

字彙 導覽解說

　　客戶對沒用過的產品，為了想要確認是否合其所需，多會讀個產品資料，但讀了心上卻還沒個踏實的感覺時，此時就需要樣品（sample）了！樣品並非都是免費的，那麼，提供的話有折扣嗎？數量可要多少？試完之後呢？這些都是在聯繫樣品事時會談到的要點，我們就抓其中的關鍵字來看看囉！

1. **試試不要錢：** 廠商最令人快意的樣品政策就是免費（for free、free of charge、at no extra charge）的啦！

2. **也大器、但得控制量：** 有些廠商會設數量限制（quantity restrictions），這可讓客戶懂得珍惜，因資源有限呢！

3. **要錢，但可便宜些：** 此時廠商會提供樣品折扣（sample discount），或對所買的第一組提供個如樣品般的額外折扣（additional discount）。

4. **試完請作答**：廠商會追蹤樣品提供的成效，會要知道客戶試用的結果如何，有的廠商就會發出個回饋表（Feedback Form），請客戶填寫。

字彙 應用搶先看：E-mail 會這麼寫！

1. Free samples are available upon the request of end users. They must fill out their lab information on the sample request form online.
   免費樣品只能提供給最終使用者，他們必須在線上的樣品要求表格裡，填上他們實驗室的相關資料。

2. We're willing to send you a sample for free of charge. Do you have a courier account? We could send a sample to you with freight collect.
   我們願意免費提供樣品給您，請問您有快遞帳號嗎？我們可以用運費到付的方式寄樣品給您。

3. Have you been able to test the sample that we sent recently to you? We'd like to hear any feedback you have.
   請問您已測試了我們最近寄給您的樣品了嗎？我們想知道一下任何您對此樣品的意見。

字彙 應用開口說：電話要這麼講！ Track 80

D ▶ Distributor 代理商　M ▶ Manufacturer 廠商

D ▶ Our customer would like to try your newly launched product to see its suitability and performance. Could you supply free samples to them?

代理商▶ 我們客戶想要試試您們新推出的產品，了解一下它合不合用、表現如何，您能提供免費樣品給他們嗎？

M ▶ Yes, we just changed our policy recently. Now we also supply free samples to customers, especially to those who are using competitors' products. We hope they will switch buying from us after trying our samples!

廠商▶ 可以的，最近我們剛改了我們的政策，現在我們也可提供免費樣品，尤其是給那些使用競爭者產品的客戶，我們希望他們在試過樣品之後，能轉而跟我們購買產品！

D ▶ That'll be a good way to attract customers and also help our promotion!

代理商▶ 那會是個吸引客戶的好方法，而且也有助我們的推廣呢！

M ▶ Yeah! But please note that only 3 free sample vials are available per end user.

廠商 ▶ 是啊！不過請注意每個使用者最多只能索取 3 組免費樣品。

D ▶ Got it! I'll tell our customer about this quantity restriction.

代理商 ▶ 了解！我會告訴我們的客戶有這項數量限制。

M ▶ Okay! Please just tell me the customer's name, institute, contact info and also the quantity they need. Then I can include the samples with your regular shipment!

廠商 ▶ 好的！您只需要告訴我客戶的名字、所屬機構、聯絡資料，還有所要的量，這樣我就可以將樣品跟著平時出給您的貨一起出囉！

 字字 計較說分明 Track 81

feedback [`fid͵bæk] *n.* 回饋、反饋的信息

例 We would certainly appreciate any feedback from you and are available to answer any of your questions at any time.

若您可給予任何的回饋訊息，我們絕對會非常感激，我們也隨時可以回答您的任何問題。

---

launch [lɔntʃ] *v.* *n.* 推出；發行

例 Click here to view all New Products launched in December 2016.

點入這裡就可看到所有在 2016 年十二月所推出的新產品。

其他字義 發射、發動、發起、展開

---

match [mætʃ] *v.* 使相配、比得上

例 Thank you for providing customer and competitor information. However, due to high production costs, we are not able to match competitor's pricing.

謝謝您提供客戶與競爭者的資訊，不過，因為生產成本高，我們沒辦法配合提供跟競爭者相同的價格。

其他字義 *n.* 比賽、火柴

performance [pə`fɔrməns]　*n.*　性能、表現、表演、績效

例 We guarantee the performance of this product for one year from the date of receipt by the end user.

我們可對此產品在使用者收貨日後一年內的品質表現提供保證。

搭配詞 performance appraisal 績效評估

---

restriction [rɪ`strɪkʃən]　*n.*　限制、限定、約束

例 The 60% discount granted for most products in this project should make up for the 25% discount restriction on the new products and our price could still be competitive.

這個案子的大多數產品我們給到 60%的折扣，應能彌補在新產品部分的 25%折扣限制，讓我們的價格還能有競爭性。

---

suitability [sutə`bɪlətɪ]　*n.*　適合、適當

例 Before utilizing the product, the user should determine the suitability of the product for its intended use.

在應用產品之前，使用者應決定此產品是否適合其預定的用途。

5-3 索取官方證明文件
Requesting Official Documents

An export **license** must be obtained...

字彙 導覽解說

Track 82

為了辦理產品登記與進出口證明這等大事，每個產業都有其各自要求的官方證明文件得去申請，不過，大致上就是要證明廠商沒問題，產品也沒問題！既然是要證明沒問題，我們就來看看幾份一般證明文件與主管機關的大名，讓我們下次見到它們時不會有問題囉！

1. **原廠掛保證：**這類證明包括了自由銷售證明（Certificate of Free Sale）、製售證明（Certificate of Manufacture and Free Sale）、登記證（Certificate of Registration）、符合 GMP 規範證明（Certificate of GMP Compliance）等。

2. **產品掛保證：**產品的官方證明有的是要證明來源，如產地證明（Certificate of Origin）、健康證明（Health Certificate）、衛生證明（Sanitary Certificate），也有核准產品可出入國境的進 / 出口許可證（Import or Export Permit / License）。

3. **誰來掛保證**：要開立證明的主管機關（authority）包括有政府各個權責機構的部（Ministry、Department）、局（Bureau）、商會（Chamber of Commerce），以及駐外代表處（Representative Office）等等。

4. **如何掛保證**：要保證，可不是一路給證明（certification）就夠，另外可還有分認證（authentication）、驗證（legalization）、公證（notarization）等等呢！

✉ 字彙 應用搶先看：E-mail 會這麼寫！

1. The U.S. Department of Commerce has our following products on the Export Control List. An export license must be obtained prior to transferring the material to an international destination. If you are interested in purchasing these products, please complete the attached Letter of Assurance Application. It takes approximately 4-6 weeks for the license to be issued.

美國商業部將我們下列產品列入出口管制清單中，這些貨品在出口前，須先取得出口證。若是您有興趣購買這些產品，請填寫附件的確認書申請表，此出口證核發約需 4～6 週。

字彙 應用開口說：電話要這麼講！ Track 83

D ▶ Distributor 代理商　M ▶ Manufacturer 廠商

D ▶ I'm glad to tell you that we've got the order for your quoted serum products!

代理商▶ 我很高興要來告訴您一件事，我們已經拿下您所報血清產品的訂單了！

M ▶ Congratulations on winning the tender!

廠商▶ 恭喜您贏得標案！

D ▶ Thanks a lot for your support on pricing! We'll place our order to you and, at the same time, we'll apply for their import permit.

代理商▶ 謝謝您在價格上的支持呢！我們會下單給您，同時，我們也會申請這些產品的進口許可證。

M ▶ Do you need us to provide any documents for the application?

廠商▶ 有需要我們這兒提供任何文件讓您去申請許可證嗎？

D ▶ Yes! Please let me have the Health Certificate for these

代理商▶ 有的！請給我這些產品的健康證明。

products.

M ▶ Okay, I'll do that. As mentioned before, at our end we also need to process the CITES[1] permit for exporting.

廠商 ▶ 好的，我會處理。先前有跟您提過，我們也得申請 CITES 許可證才能出口。

D ▶ Yes, I do remember that! How long will it take you to get the documents issued by these authorities?

代理商 ▶ 是的，我還記得！那需要多久才能拿到這些主管機關核發的文件呢？

M ▶ It takes approximately 80-90 days for us to receive these export documents. After application, I'll keep you updated on the progress!

廠商 ▶ 大概要 80～90天後我們才會收到這些出口文件。等申請之後，如果有任何進展的消息，我就會馬上告訴您！

註[1]：CITES: Convention on International Trade in Endangered Species of Wild Fauna and Flora / 瀕臨絕種野生動植物國際貿易公約

字字 計較說分明

 Track 84

authority [ə`θɔrətɪ] *n.* 管理機構

例 We need a "Letter of no objection" issued by the appropriate competent national authority.

我們需要一份國家主管機關所出具的「無異議信函」。

其他字義 權力、當局、權威、影響力

相關字 authorize [`ɔθə͵raɪz] *v.*

....

certificate [sə`tɪfəkɪt] *n.* 證明書、執照

例 Once you receive your import permit you need to send us a copy because the wording on the DEFRA[2] Certificate must be the same as on your import permit.

等您一收到進口許可證，就必須馬上寄影本給我們，因為 DEFRA 證明裡頭的用語得要跟您們進口許可證所寫的一樣。

其他字義 [sə`tɪfə͵ket] *v.* 發證書證明

註[2]：DEFRA: Department for Environment, Food and Rural Affairs ／英 國環境、食品與鄉村事務部

....

chamber [`tʃembɚ] *n.* 會所、議院

例 These commercial documents may need to be authenticated by a Chamber of Commerce.

這些商業文件得要經由商會認證。

其他字義 室、房間

license [`laɪsns]   *n.*   許可證、執照、許可

例 The Export License is attached for your records. It is valid through June 30, 2019.

附上出口許可證供您留做紀錄，其效期至 2019 年 6 月 30 日。

notarize [`notə͵raɪz]   *v.*   公證

例 You have to have the documents notarized by a Notary to validate them, so they will be accepted by our authorities.

這些文件得要經由公證人辦理公證，予以證實，這樣我們的主管機關才會接受這些文件。

registration [͵rɛdʒɪ`streʃən]   *n.*   登記、註冊

例 A copy of your business registration certificate will be required to complete the registration process.

必須要有您的商業登記證影本，才能完成註冊程序。

相關字 register *[`rɛdʒɪstɚ]*   *v.*

5-4 到貨問題
Faulty on Arrival

If you find that your goods are **faulty** on arrival...

🌐 **字彙 導覽解說**

　　貨好不容易盼來了、送到了眼前，但卻發現有缺貨、出錯或到貨損壞這些出貨問題，那可真是會讓人急得跳腳呢！雖然你的腳忙著跳，但手也千萬別閒著，得要趕忙跟廠商這樣子反應囉：

1. **有缺**：若是貨來得不全，組件有少（missing components、lost parts），到了還是跟沒到一樣，用不了，就得請廠商快快補出貨了。

2. **出錯**：若所出的貨有誤（wrong item），那就會牽涉到退貨（return）、換貨（exchange）的處理了。而有些產品因退運不划算（uneconomical），或是退回也無法使用，那廠商會請買方就另做他用，或是乾脆就丟棄（dispose）吧！

3. **到貨瑕疵、損壞**：若來貨有瑕疵（are faulty、have defects）、到貨損壞（Damage on Arrival），或是有明顯

的、功能上的問題（visible / functional defects），那就得要退換貨了！

字彙 應用搶先看：E-mail 會這麼寫！

1. If you find that your goods are faulty on arrival, then you are entitled to a repair, a replacement or a refund.
若您發現貨品到貨有瑕疵，您有權要求修理、補出貨或退款。

2. If you discover that your goods are visibly damaged on arrival, please contact us within 7 days with details of the damage. We'll then arrange to ship a replacement to you.
若您收到貨後發現有明顯損壞的情況，請在七天內跟我們聯絡，並請提供損壞的詳細資訊，然後我們就會安排寄出替換的貨給您。

3. In the event that any of our products are faulty, damaged on arrival or incompatibility, we requires you to return the goods to us for examination, after which a refund or a replacement will be issued.
若有到貨瑕疵、損壞，或是不相容的問題，請您退回貨品供我們檢測，檢測後我們就會核發退款或寄出替換品項。

 Track 86

字彙 應用開口說：電話要這麼講！

D ▶ Distributor 代理商   **M** ▶ Manufacturer 廠商

D ▶ We just received the box sent from you last Friday but found that its inner bottles have cracks!

代理商 ▶ 我們剛收到您上星期五寄出的那箱貨，但發現裡頭的瓶子有裂耶！

M ▶ Really? We've never had this problem with any other customer... Can you take photos of them and send them to me?

廠商 ▶ 真的嗎？我們倒是從沒聽過其他客戶反應過這樣的問題……，您可不可照幾張照片發給我？

D ▶ No problem! In fact, I've already taken several of them. I'll send them to you later. Do you still need me to return the whole kit to you?

代理商 ▶ 沒問題，實際上我已經拍了好幾張了，等一下就發給您。那您有要我把整組退回給您嗎？

M ▶ No, that'll be too costly to return. You could just discard

廠商 ▶ 不用，退運成本太高了，您可以就把有裂的瓶子

the bottles with cracks and use the other components as you wish.

丟掉，其他的組件您想怎麼用都好。

D ▶ Okay! So when can you send us a replacement kit?

代理商 ▶ 好的！所以您什麼時候會寄補出的產品組給我們呢？

M ▶ After receiving your photos, we'll identify what we can do to make sure the same problem does not happen again. About the replacement kit, I think I can send it to you this Friday!

廠商 ▶ 等收到您拍的照片之後，我們會看看能怎麼做，以確保同樣的問題不會再發生。至於補出的貨，我想我可以在這個星期五出貨給您！

字字 計較說分明

Track 87

damage [`dæmɪdʒ]   *n.*   *v.*   損害

例 Please inspect the product on arrival and notify us in writing of any claims for shortages, defects, or damages.

請在貨到後檢查一下，若有任何短缺、瑕疵或損壞的情況，請以書面方式通知我們。

---

defect [dɪ`fɛkt]   *n.*   缺點、瑕疵

例 Buyer shall promptly notify Seller in writing upon the discovery of any defect. Buyer may return the defective Products to Seller with all related costs prepaid by Buyer first.

買方若發現有任何瑕疵，應立即以書面方式通知賣方，而買方可將瑕疵品退回賣方，所有相關成本須先由買方預付。

---

discard [dɪs`kɑrd]   *v.*   丟棄

例 Please use these updated questionnaire forms from now on and discard the older versions.

從現在開始，請使用這些新版的問卷表格，舊版表格就請捨棄不用。

---

exchange [ɪks`tʃendʒ] *n.* *v.* 交換

例 Your complete satisfaction with our products is guaranteed and items may be returned or exchanged within thirty days from when it was shipped.

我們保證會讓您對我們的產品有絕對的滿意，在出貨後三十天內，都可辦理退貨或換貨。

faulty [`fɔltɪ] *adj.* 有缺點的、有瑕疵的

例 Where a product has been made to measure for you, unless faulty, we're unable to refund or offer an exchange.

若是為您量身訂做的產品，除非有瑕疵，否則我們不接受退貨或替換。

replacement [rɪ`plesmənt] *n.* 代替、代替物

例 Any battery failure beyond 14 days is not eligible for replacement under product warranty.

電池在 14 天後如有任何異常狀況，雖在產品保固期裡，但仍不符合替換替換品的條件。

5-5 保固服務 Warranty

We shall repair the defective
product covered by the **warranty**.

字彙 導覽解說

　　說到保固服務這事兒，首先買方會問的就是保固期有多長，在買方看著長長的期間而點頭稱是的同時，廠商就會再送上一些限制條件，告訴你哪些情形不在保固範圍之內，請買方可要好好注意一下哩！

1. **保固起跑**：產品保固（warranty）的起算點多是看買方的購買日（the date of purchase），而有的設備產品則是自買方完成線上登錄註冊（register）後開始算起。

2. **保固什麼**：要保固當然是要保證產品不會發生問題（free of defects），若有問題，則會免費修理（repair）或換掉（replace）有問題的產品。

3. **不符保固**：保固服務也是有限制（restrictions）的，若因使用者操作上疏忽（negligence）、使用不當（improper

use、misuse）、意外損傷（being damaged by accident），或是不當維護（improper maintenance）這些原因而導致故障，就超出了保固責任（warranty obligation），此時修理或換貨就沒得享有免費待遇了！

字彙 應用搶先看：E-mail 會這麼寫！

1. We shall repair or replace the defective product covered by the warranty and warrant the products free of defect in material and workmanship under normal use during the warranty period.

   對於保固範圍裡發現有瑕疵的產品，我們會提供修理與換貨的服務，並於保固期間內正常使用的條件之下，保證產品在材料與工藝技術上不會發生故障。

2. The warranty does not apply if the faults were caused by negligent handling of the product, improper use together with products that were not produced by us, modified use or use other than in accordance with the operating instructions.

   若因如下行為而導致故障，則不適用保固服務，這些行為包括產品操作上有疏忽的情況、搭配其他非我們生產產品的不當使用、改裝使用，或是其他不符操作指示規定的使用情形。

 **字彙 應用開口說：電話要這麼講！** Track 89

D ▶ Distributor 代理商　**M** ▶ Manufacturer 廠商

D ▶ Our customer encountered a breakdown on your product. I'd like to check with you whether this product is still covered under warranty.

代理商 ▶ 我們客戶使用您們的產品後發現有故障狀況，我想跟您查一下這個產品是否還在保固期裡。

M ▶ Not a problem! Please tell me the product serial no., so I can check the warranty status and find out when it expires.

廠商 ▶ 沒問題！請告訴我產品的序號，這樣我就可查它的保固狀況，看看保固是哪時候到期。

D ▶ Okay. Its serial no. 960925.

代理商 ▶ 好的，它的序號是 960925。

M ▶ Wait a moment... Yes, it's still under warranty until June 30, 2017. So how can I help you?

廠商 ▶ 請等一下……，是的，這產品還在保固期期間裡，到 2017 年6 月 30 號才會到期。那您要我怎麼協助您呢？

D ▶ I've checked the product by following the troubleshooting steps listed in the Operating Manual but the problem still can't be solved.

代理商▶ 我有檢查了這個產品，有照著操作手冊上的問題解決步驟來做，但還是沒辦法解決問題。

M ▶ I see. You could return the product for our examination. I'll e-mail a RMA[1] no. to you for you to process the return shipment.

廠商▶ 瞭解，您可以將產品退回給我們檢查，我會再 e-mail 退貨授權號碼給您，讓您辦理退貨。

註[1]：全名為 Return Material Authorization，5-6 與 5-7 單元有更多説明喔！

 字字 計較說分明 Track 90

extend [ɪk`stɛnd]　*v.*　延長、延伸

例 Following annual calibration, overhaul or repair, the product warranty will be extended for a further 12 months.

若有每年校正、全面檢查或維修，則此產品保固期可延長 12 個月。

---

maintenance [`mentənəns]　*n.*　保養維修、維持

例 This warranty is not transferable and excludes routine maintenance, consumables, and parts subject to normal wear and tear.

此保固服務無法移轉，亦不包含定期保養維修、消耗品，以及會正常耗損的零件。

相關字 maintain *[men`ten]*　*v.*

---

negligence [`nɛglɪdʒəns]　*n.*　疏忽

例 This warranty does not cover damages or defects caused by negligence, improper use, and assembly of parts or accessories that are not original.

此保固並不涵蓋因疏忽、不當使用及組裝非原有零件或配件而導致的損壞與故障。

---

obligation [ˌɑblə`geʃən]   *n.*   責任、義務

例 Our warranty obligation starts on the date of the purchase of a new product.

我們的保固責任始於新品購買日當天。

....

troubleshooting [trʌblˌʃutɪŋ]   *n.*   問題解決、故障排除

例 This section covers troubleshooting information which should help you solve the majority of problems.

這個部分包含了問題解決的資料，應有助您解決大部分的問題。

....

warranty [`wɔrəntɪ]   *n.*   保固、擔保

例 The warranty will be invalidated if any of the terms and conditions of the warranty are not adhered to, including incorrect installation of the product.

若是沒有遵照保固條款的規定，包括像是產品安裝不當，那麼保固將會失效。

相關字 warrant *[`wɔrənt]*   *v.*   保證（貨物的）品質

5-6 退貨政策 Return Policy

Products may be returned with our
permission...

字彙 導覽解說　　　　　　　　　　　○ Track 91

　　廠商的退貨規定可以有兩極化的不同表現，一種是乾乾脆脆的「不給退」，另一種就是落落長的限制條件了！不給退有其理由，給退但設限也有其邏輯，我們這就一併來跑個兩極，見個世面囉！

1. **沒有退路**：有的貨品屬於不可退貨的品項（Non-Returnable Items），既已出貨，就不能再退回給廠商了！

2. **拒收**：廠商可接受退貨，但若不按照規定來，像是沒先申請退貨授權號碼（Return Material Authorization No.、Return Code）、沒事先得到廠商的許可（permission）、包裝不當（improper packaging）、沒有保險（uninsured）、超過接受退貨天數、退貨貨品不全或是少了證明等附件，就算貨都送到了廠商處，廠商還是可拒收呢！

3. 衍生費用：廠商收到退貨要整理、要送回倉庫，也是增加了成本，因此多數廠商會對退貨收取重新上架費（restocking fee），以補退貨整理及重入倉儲的成本囉！

字彙 應用搶先看：E-mail 會這麼寫！

1. Please note that to be eligible for return, items must be in their original purchase condition, include all product documentation, and be shipped within 30 days.

請注意，若要合乎退貨規定，產品須以其原購買時的狀態退回，包括所有產品文件，且要在 30 天內寄出。

2. If your customer doesn't want to keep the product, then you could ask them to return to us, given that it has been properly stored this entire time.

若是您的客戶不想留著這項產品，那麼您可以退給我們，不過先決條件是在這段期間裡，產品都有適當儲存著。

3. Products may not be returned except with our permission, and then only in strict compliance with our return shipment instructions. Any returned items will be subject to a 15 percent restocking fee.

貨品若未經我們許可則不得退回，且須嚴格符合我們的退運指示。任何退回的貨品皆須支付 15%的重新上架費。

字彙 應用開口說：電話要這麼講！ Track 92

D ▶ Distributor 代理商 M ▶ Manufacturer 廠商

D ▶ I've received the shipment but just found that I accidentally ordered the wrong product! Can I return it to you?

代理商▶ 我已經收到了貨，但剛剛發現有一個產品訂錯了！我可以退給您們嗎？

M ▶ Yes, you can! All of our products can be returned under our Return Policy.

廠商▶ 可以的！我們的退貨政策是所有的產品都可以退貨的。

D ▶ Return Policy? Could you tell me more about it?

代理商▶ 退貨政策？您可以多說明一些嗎？

M ▶ Sure! All products are eligible for return within 14 working days from the date of receipt as long as they're sent back in unused condition and in their original packaging.

廠商▶ 當然！只要貨還未使用，原有包裝還在，在收貨日後 14 個工作天內都可以退貨。

D ▶ Whoops! I just unpacked the product's box...

代理商 ▶ 啊！我剛打開了產品的盒子耶⋯⋯。

M ▶ That's okay. But please make sure that all the accessories and enclosed documents are returned as well.

廠商 ▶ 那沒關係，但是請確定所有的配件和所附的文件都會一起退回。

D ▶ I'll do that! Are there any other instructions?

代理商 ▶ 我會照辦！還有別的指示嗎？

M ▶ Yeah! Please note that you have to bear the cost of returning the goods and there will be a restocking fee of 15 percent.

廠商 ▶ 有喔！請注意您得負擔退貨的成本，而且還會有15%的重新上架費。

D ▶ Okay! Thanks for all the information!

代理商 ▶ 好的！謝謝您告訴我這些資訊！

 Track 93

字字 計較說分明

compliance [kəm`plaɪəns] *n.* 符合、順從

例 In compliance with our return policy, we will issue a refund to you within 14 days of receipt.

若符合我們的退貨政策，我們就會在收貨後 14 天內退款給您。

相關字 comply *[kəm`plaɪ]* *v.*

---

eligible [`ɛlɪdʒəbl̩] *adj.* 有資格的

例 To be eligible for a return, the product must be unused and in the same condition that you received it including all extras and free items provided. It must also be in the original packaging.

要符合退貨的條件，產品必須尚未使用，須與收貨時狀況相同，也要包括所有的附贈品項，亦須以原包裝退回。

---

permission [pɚ`mɪʃən] *n.* 允許、許可、同意

例 Any item found unsatisfactory may be returned within 7 days with our permission.

若有任何不滿意的產品，經我們許可後，都可在七天內退貨。

相關字 permit *[pɚ`mɪt]* *v.*

policy [`pɑləsɪ］　*n.*　政策

例 If an item is returned but not complying with our Return Policy, we will not refund you.

若是有貨退回但不符我們退貨政策的規定，我們就無法退款給您。

refuse [rɪ`fjuz]　*v.*　拒絕

例 Returns without our return code, insurance or proper packages will be refused upon receipt.

若退貨沒有寫上我們的退貨碼、沒有保險，或是包裝不當，我們就會拒收。

相關字 refusal *[rɪ`fjuzl]*　*n.*

restock [ri`stɑk]　*v.*　（為……）重新進貨

例 The seller can charge a reasonable restocking fee, up to 20% if the product is returned in the same condition.

若產品以其原有的狀況退回，賣方可收取一個合理的重新上架費，費率可達 20%。

5-7 辦理退貨
Return Shipment

All **returns** must be **authorized** by an RMA Number.

字彙 導覽解說　　　　　　　　　　Track 94

　　退貨的要求會發生在出錯貨、訂錯貨、到貨損壞或其他的狀況之下，而貨物好不容易一路到了買方的手上，要再送它一路回到廠商處，可也有好幾個要打點的關卡呢！

1. **要有退貨授權（Return Material Authorization / RMA）才可退**：大多數的廠商會要買方說明退貨原因，待其審視、核准後，就會給買方一個退貨授權號碼（RMA No. / Code），買方退貨時，也一定要隨貨附上退貨授權書。

2. **包裝**：有的廠商會要求以原包裝（original packaging）退回，若貨物出口時有特殊溫度控制，退回時當然也要比照辦理。

3. **退貨文件**：所退之貨並無銷售之實（No sale or transaction），所以在退貨中的商業發票上會要求註明，也

會要求加註當初出貨的提單號碼，並寫上所列金額為僅供海關參考之用（for customs reference / purposes only）。

✉字彙 應用搶先看：E-mail 會這麼寫！

1. All returns must be authorized by an RMA Number. Please email your request for authorization number before shipping back any merchandise.
   所有退貨皆須有 RMA 退貨授權號碼，在您退回任何貨給我們之前，請寫 email 給我們，要求授權號碼。

2. When processing the return shipment, please make sure to indicate the following in the comments section of the Commercial Invoice:
   ・This product was originally shipped to Taiwan via FedEx AWB no. 805726811202.
   ・No sale / transaction has occurred.
   ・The value stated is for Customs purposes only.
   當辦理退貨時，請確實在商業發票的備註欄裡註明下列事項：
   ・此產品原出口至台灣的 FedEx 提單號碼為 805726811202。
   ・無銷售／交易發生。
   ・所列的金額僅供海關參考之用。

 **字彙** 應用開口說：電話要這麼講！ Track 95

M ▸ Manufacturer 廠商   D ▸ Distributor 代理商

M ▸ I got your e-mail just now saying that you're going to arrange the return shipment to us today, right?

廠商 ▸ 我剛收到您的 e-mail，說今天會寄出退貨給我們，是嗎？

D ▸ Yeah! We're now making its shipping documents. FedEx will come pick up the parcel later today.

代理商 ▸ 是的！我們現在正在準備出貨文件，FedEx 今天稍晚會來取包裹。

M ▸ I'd like to remind you to send the product back in its original box and pack it with a minimum of 30lbs of dry ice.

廠商 ▸ 我想要提醒您一下，退回的貨要用原包裝的箱子，也請放至少 30 磅的乾冰。

D ▸ Dry ice is no problem. But about the box, we've already packed it in a similar insulated box. Is that okay?

代理商 ▸ 乾冰沒問題，但是關於箱子的部分，我們已經用了個類似的絕緣箱打包了，這樣可以嗎？

M ▶ That's fine! You know the product is sensitive to temperature. We just want to make sure a suitable box is used.

廠商 ▶ 也可以！您知道這個產品對溫度敏感，我們只是要確認有用適合的箱子出貨罷了。

D ▶ You can rest assured about that! We'll follow all the instructions written on your Return Authorization Letter.

代理商 ▶ 請放心！我們會照著您退貨授權書上頭寫的所有指示來做的。

M ▶ That's great! Please remember to tell me the tracking no. once you get it.

廠商 ▶ 太好了！等您一拿到追蹤號碼，請記得馬上告訴我！

Part 5 客服與客訴

字字 計較說分明

authorization [ˌɔθərəˈzeʃən] *n.* 授權、批准

例 Please see an updated letter of authorization attached per your request.

依您的要求，在此附上更新的授權書。

相關字 authorize [ˈɔθəˌraɪz] *v.*

---

material [məˈtɪrɪəl] *n.* 物質、原料； *adj.* 物質的

例 Since the product is a temperature sensitive material, it will need to be returned on Mondays so that we can receive it during week days.

因為這項產品屬於對溫度敏感的物質，所以退貨得排在星期一，這樣我們才能在週間收到貨。

---

merchandise [ˈmɝtʃənˌdaɪz] *n.* 商品、貨物

例 Returned merchandise must include all original components and packaging in the same saleable condition in which it was received.

所退回的貨品須包含所有原有配件與包裝，須與收貨時的可銷售狀態相同。

return [rɪ`tɝn] *v.* *n.* 退貨

例 For these items, there is a no-return policy once you receive shipment. Please keep that in mind when deciding to order.

這些產品在您收了貨之後，按規定就不得退貨了，請您在決定下單時考慮這一點。

---

traceable [`tresəbl̩] *adj.* 可追蹤的

例 Please use a traceable method when returning your item as we cannot accept liability if something is lost in transit and fails to reach us.

退貨時請以可追蹤的分式來辦理，若貨物在運送途中遺失，以至於我們沒有收到貨，我們將無法負責。

---

transit [`trænsɪt] *n.* 運輸、運送、通過、過境

例 Damage arising from insufficient packaging or mishandling in transit is the responsibility of customers.

在運送途中若因包裝不足或處理不當，導致貨品損壞，則屬客戶之責任。

其他字義 *v.* 轉運、通過

5-8 退款 Refund

We recommend returning for a **refund**...

字彙 導覽解說

　　若有退貨或是廠商多收了錢，後續處理就有可能牽涉到退款（refund）。說到退款，重點不外乎會用何方式將錢「退」給買方，是實際退錢到買方帳戶嗎？還是要開立個貸項通知單（Credit Memo、Credit Note）來處理？另一個要點就是看可退的「款」有多少了！我們這就進一步來談談怎麼「退」一筆囉！

1. **怎麼辦理退款**：若是真要退錢，退款的方式通常會是比照買方付款方式，怎麼來怎麼退！廠商會要買方提出要求（request），有的廠商還要求買方要有書面通知（written notice）的程序才會受理、處理（process），之後廠商就會進行（proceed）退款程序，核發（issue）退款。

2. **什麼費用不能退**：買方所支付的發票總額，除了產品成本之外，通常還包括了處理手續費（handling fee / charge）、包

裝費（packaging fee / charge），以及相關稅負（taxes、duties）等其他費用，而這些費用都是無法退款的 （non-refundable）。

📧 字彙 應用搶先看：E-mail 會這麼寫！

1. Your Credit Memo is attached. You can use it as a deduction for future payments or use it to request a refund.
在此附上您的貸項通知單，您可以在下次付款時扣除此金額，或是用其來要求退款。

2. To expedite exchanging for different product, we recommend returning for a refund and placing a new order. Please allow approximately 2 weeks for your refund to be processed.
為了要加速替換另一項產品給您，我們建議您辦理退貨、退款，另外再下一份新訂單給我們。我們約需兩個星期的時間來處理退款。

3. If you do not accept the Terms and Conditions of Sale, please contact us to arrange for an immediate return of this un-opened product for a full refund.
若是您不接受我們的銷售條款，請與我們連絡，將您尚未開箱的產品立刻退回給我們，以辦理全額退款。

字彙 應用開口說：電話要這麼講！ Track 98

C ▶ Customer 客戶　　**M** ▶ Manufacturer 廠商

C ▶ Hi, I've received the Invoice for my recent order. You said you'd give me a special discount of 20% off, but it's still the list price that was invoiced!

客戶 ▶ 嗨，我有收到了我最近這一份訂單的發票了，您有說會給我 20％的折扣，不過發票所收的金額還是定價耶！

M ▶ Ah... I forgot to adjust the pricing! Please accept my sincere apologies for the oversight!

廠商 ▶ 啊……，我忘了調整價格了！真的很抱歉有這個疏忽！

C ▶ That's okay! Please just correct it.

客戶 ▶ 沒關係的！請幫我調整就好。

M ▶ Sure! Would you like us to refund or leave this as an open credit memo on your account?

廠商 ▶ 當然！那請問您要退款，還是要留個貸項通知單的款項在您的帳戶呢？

C ▶ I prefer you refund it. By the

客戶 ▶ 我想請您辦理退款。

way, how long will it take to refund us?

對了，您退款給我們需要多少時間呢？

M ▶ The way you originally paid for the order will determine how you are refunded. So... How did you pay us?

廠商 ▶ 您的訂單原先是用什麼方式付款的，我們就會以同樣的方式退款給您。所以……，您是怎樣付款的呢？

C ▶ I paid by credit card.

客戶 ▶ 我是用信用卡付款的。

M ▶ Okay. We will refund your credit card with the difference!

廠商 ▶ 好的，那我們就會將差價金額退到您的信用卡！

字字 計較說分明

Track 99

deduct [dɪ`dʌkt] *v.* 扣除、減除

例 Any return postage or courier's administration fees incurred will be deducted from the amount refunded to you.

任何退貨所產生的郵資或快遞行政費用，都將會從退給您的金額中扣除。

---

notice [`notɪs] *n.* 通知、公告

例 If you decide to cancel the transaction, you must give to us a written notice of cancellation.

若您決定要取消交易，您得給我們個取消的書面通知。

相關字 notify [`notə͵faɪ] *v.* 通知；notification [͵notəfə`keʃən] *n.* 通知、通告

---

originally [ə`rɪdʒənḷɪ] *adv.* 原來地、起初地

例 If you paid by credit or debit card, we'll refund the same card originally used to place and pay for the order.

若您是以信用卡或金融卡支付貨款，那麼我們的退款就會退至您原本用來付款的同一張卡片中。

reduce [rɪ`djus]　*v.*　減少

例 Please note we will reduce your refund to reflect any reduction in the value of the products, if this has been caused by inappropriate handling.

請注意一下，若有任何因不當處理而導致產品價值減損，我們就會減少要退給您的金額，以反映價值減損的部分。

refundable [rɪ`fʌndəbḷ]　*adj.*　可退還的

例 Only the cost of the goods and standard shipping are refundable. Where alternative shipping is selected and paid for, shipping will only be refunded to the value of standard shipping.

只有貨品的成本與標準運費可退款，若所選所付的是別種運送方式的話，則可退的運費只計算到標準運費的金額。

responsibility [rɪˌspɑnsə`bɪlətɪ]　*n.*　責任、負擔

例 All shipping costs are the responsibility of customers. So you need to prepay the freight charges to and from destination.

所有運費皆須由客戶負擔，所以您須預付退貨來回的運費。

5-9 罰款 Penalty

There will be a x % **penalty** per day for delivery delay.

字彙 導覽解說

Track 100

　　若買賣雙方談到罰款，那事情就有點兒嚴重啦！一定有約（合約）在先，而且失約了！買賣不成仁義在，賣了貨但貨還不來就有罰款在啦！對於這麼重要的事，説明起來可有好些搭配使用的字，我們這就來從「罰」計議囉！

1. **為何開罰**：合約（contract）上設定了交貨日期，若有任何交貨延遲（delivery delay）或是貨到了但有驗收（acceptance）過不了的情況發生，就是違反（breach）了合約規定，有的合約就會配套訂出罰款（penalty、fine）規定。

2. **怎麼罰**：開罰的計價標的多半是訂單金額（order amount）的一個百分比，依延遲日數累計罰款，但這樣的延遲也不是光靠罰款就可一路延下去，若是貨真的就不來，那連訂單、合約都要取消（cancel）、要失效（null、void）了，但不要

以為訂單取消就沒事，合約上多半還會訂出相應的罰金規定，重罰取消合約這等大代誌呢！

字彙 應用搶先看：E-mail 會這麼寫！

1. The products should arrive on site ready for our in-house installation teams to get started before the delivery deadline. There will be a 1% penalty per day for delivery delay. The first 1% deduction starts immediately the day after the deadline.

   貨品應在交貨期限前送抵我們的所在處，且應已準備就緒，可供我們內部安裝團隊開始作業。若有交貨延遲的情況發生，則將收取訂單金額的 1%為每日罰金，從期限後一天立刻開始起算。

2. The penalty amount is limited to a maximum of 10% of the amount of the order. In case of a delivery delay in excess of 4 weeks, we are entitled to declare the order null and void without any cost being charged for this.

   罰款金額以訂單金額的 10%為上限，若交貨延遲的時間超過 4 個星期，那麼我們將有權宣稱此訂單無效，且也不能對我們收取任何費用。

字彙 應用開口說：電話要這麼講！ Track 101

D ▶ Distributor 代理商　　**M** ▶ Manufacturer 廠商

D ▶ Hi, I'm calling to check with you about our pending order. Have you got any updated news?

代理商 ▶ 嗨，我打來是要問問我們那一份還沒出貨的訂單的狀況，請問您有什麼新的消息嗎？

M ▶ I do... But I'm sorry! It's not good news... Unfortunately, there is a production delay and it will not be ready until mid June...

廠商 ▶ 確實有……，但抱歉，不是好消息……，這項產品生產有延遲，應該要到六月中才會有貨……。

D ▶ Oh! That'll be too late... The delivery deadline stipulated on that contract is May 31st.

代理商 ▶ 喔！但那樣就太晚了……，合約上列的交貨期限是 5 月 31 日。

M ▶ It's nearly impossible for us to meet the deadline... .

廠商 ▶ 我們幾乎是不太可能在期限之前交貨……。

D ▶ So... We'll be fined for the

代理商 ▶ 那麼的話……，我

delivery delay...

們就會因交貨遲延而被罰款……。

M ▶ Do you know how the penalty will be calculated?

廠商 ▶ 您知道罰款是怎麼計算的嗎？

D ▶ Yes, I know that a daily penalty of 1% of order amount will be charged.

代理商 ▶ 是的，我知道每天是罰訂單金額的1%。

M ▶ Got it! We'll make every effort to get the product released earlier so as to lower the penalty!

廠商 ▶ 瞭解！我們會盡力將這個產品早點生產出來，這樣也就能降低罰款的金額了！

 **字字** 計較說分明

breach [britʃ]   *n.*   違反

例 Breach of contract can occur if any of the agreed terms and conditions of a contract are broken.

若是有不遵守任何同意條款的情況發生，就是違反了合約。

搭配詞 breach of confidentiality agreement 違反保密協定；breach of duty 失職；breach of trust 背信

---

deadline [ˋdɛdˌlaɪn]   *n.*   最後期限

例 I think we might fail to meet the customer's expectation and might miss the deadline!

我想我們可能會達不到客戶的期望，可能無法按時完成。

---

fine [faɪn]   *n. v.*   罰款

例 As specified in the terms and conditions, we'll be fined $ 5,000 for breach of contract.

如在條款中所指明，我們違約的話就要被罰以$ 5,000 的罰款。

impose [ɪm`poz]　*v.*　徵（稅）、強行收取

例 Penalty is the punishment imposed for breaking a rule, law, or contract.

罰款就是在有違反規則、法律或合約時所加諸的處罰。

---

null [nʌl]　*adj.*　無效的；　*v.*　使無效

例 If the conditions of the contract are not fulfilled, then the contract will be null and void

若是沒有履行合約條件的話，那此合約將會無效。

相關字 nullify [`nʌlə͵faɪ]　*v.*　使無效

---

penalty [`pɛnḷtɪ]　*n.*　罰款、處罰

例 We need to pay a late delivery penalty of 0.1% per day of the total value.

我們得要支付延遲交貨的罰款，每日罰款金額為總額的 1%。

相關字 penalize [`pinḷ͵aɪz]　*v.*　處罰

6-1 業務會議
Sales Meeting

Please see the tentative **agenda** for our conference...

字彙 導覽解說

Track 103

　　廠商與代理商多會定期舉行業務會議，以瞭解雙方各自供給與需求面的市場狀況。這類會議很重要，談的也都是要事，那到底會談到哪些主題？該準備的開會資料有哪些？我們這就來看看若要上場開會，該要備什麼而來囉！

1. **業績有多少**：業務會議當然要來個業績檢討（sales review），說說做到的業績（sales、turnover、sales volume、sales performance），抓出成長率（growth rate），看看業績目標（sales target）的達成率，有了這些數字，那就知道這場會議可挺著胸笑笑談，還是咬著牙刻苦談囉！

2. **市場知多少**：要苦幹實幹也要先知道市場狀況（market status）才有用，得要知道市場趨勢（trend）、競爭者（competitor）、客戶端的需求（demand），以及面臨的挑戰（challenge）有哪些。

3. **計策有多精彩**：守成不易，攻下山頭也是難，不論是何情

況，都一定得大談特談行銷（marketing）與推廣、促銷的（promotional）策略（Strategy）、戰術（tactic）、計畫（plan）這些謀略了！

✉ 字彙 應用搶先看：E-mail 會這麼寫！

1. <u>Please see the tentative agenda for our conference call</u> below. If you wish to add anything to the agenda, please just let me know. Thanks! <u>請看下列針對我們電話會議所暫定的議程</u>，如您想要加上其他事項，就再請告訴我，謝謝！

   ・Sales review 業務檢討：

   Sales performance 業績表現

   Sales target 業績目標

   Growth rate 成長率

   ・Market Review 市場檢討 ：

   Market share 市佔率

   Competitors 競爭者

   Challenges and risks 挑戰與風險

   ・Marketing 行銷：

   Success stories 成功案例

   Target customers 目標客戶

   New product lines 新產品線

   Strategies and plans 策略與計畫

   Exhibition plans 展覽計畫

字彙 應用開口說：電話要這麼講！ Track 104

M ▶ Manufacturer 廠商　　**D ▶** Distributor 代理商

M ▶ Hi, yesterday I sent the agenda for our conference call next Wednesday. Did you receive that?

廠商▶ 嗨，我昨天有發了我們下星期三電話會議的議程給您了，您有收到嗎？

D ▶ Yeah, I did! We had an internal meeting this morning discussing the topics you mentioned!

代理商▶ 有的，我們今天早還開了個內部會議，討論您所提到的主題呢！

M ▶ I'm glad to hear that! I believe we'll have a productive meeting!

廠商 ▶ 很高興聽到您這麼說！我相信我們一定會有個很有收穫的會議呢！

D ▶ That's for sure! Hah! By the way, we'd like to add items to the agenda.

代理商▶ 一定的啊！哈！對了，我們想加些主題到議程裡。

M ▶ Sure! Please just tell me!

廠商▶ 當然可以！請說！

D ▶ Okay! We also want to discuss the discounts that you could offer us for key projects.

代理商 ▶ 好的！我們也想要討論一下您對重要案子可給我們的折扣。

M ▶ No problem! We used to offer discounts case by case. Maybe we could discuss that further to get a whole picture of our discount policy.

廠商 ▶ 沒問題，先前我們是個案談，可能也可以就我們折扣政策的整體來談。

D ▶ Yes, that's what we want to see!

代理商 ▶ 沒錯，這就是我們想要的！

Part 6 ｜ 業務與行銷

 Track 105

agenda [ə`dʒɛndə]　*n.*　議程

例 The agenda for the webinar will be provided at a later date.

線上研討會的議程會在幾天後提供。

相關字 agendum *[ə`dʒɛndəm]* 待辦事項

---

challenge [`tʃælɪndʒ]　*n.*　*v.*　挑戰

例 All firms face the challenge of a changing market with complex trends.

所有的公司都面臨了市場不停變動、不斷有複雜發展趨勢的挑戰。

---

review [rɪ`vju]　*n.*　*v.*　再檢查、回顧

例 We have recently reviewed your sales performance and noticed that you have not purchased any of our new version products as yet this year.

我們最近有看了您的銷售業績，發現您今年都沒有訂購我們新版的產品。

strategy [`strætədʒɪ] *n.* 策略、戰略

例 We could help develop successful sales strategies and gain access to new markets and customers.

我們可以幫您想出成功的銷售策略，讓您得以進入新市場，找到新客戶。

相關字 strategical *[strə`tidʒɪkḷ]* *adj.* = strategic *[strə`tidʒɪk]* *adj.*

---

tactic [`tæktɪk] *n.* 戰術、策略、對策

例 Please share with us any examples of a successful sales tactic you have used or seen elsewhere.

請跟大家分享任何您有用過或看到過的成功銷售對策。

比較 tactics *[`tæktɪks]* 戰術、用兵學

---

turnover [`tɝn͵ovɚ] *n.* 營業額

例 We expect the increase of your turnover in 2017 to be 60.000,00 EUR. This is the condition for signing the exclusive distribution agreement for next year.

我們希望您 2017 的營業額能增加到 6 萬歐元，這是明年可簽獨家代理合約的條件。

6-2 安排會議
Arrange a Meeting

We'd like to schedule a conference call to discuss...

字彙 導覽解說 Track 106

　　要開會，就得要「約」會，要好好策畫、安排一下會議的人事時地。當年要開會、要看到對方，一定得碰頭，而現在拜通訊科技之賜，遙遠兩地的雙方可一起來開個電話會議或視訊會議，有實效又有時效！而約會的方式不同，牽涉到的安排事項就不一樣了，我們這就來挑些關鍵字來看看囉！

1. **碰面促膝**：要真的碰頭，人就要飛洋過海，於是就會談到班機行程（flight schedule）、住宿（accommodation）與接機（pick-up）安排。

2. **空中相會**：電話會議（teleconference、conference call）的舉行方式有好幾種，包括有多方通話（multi-participant phone calls）和視訊會議（video conference）。要邀請對方來開電話會議，告訴對方要撥打的電話號碼（dial-in number），或是請對方將你的 Skype 帳號加入聯絡人清單（Contacts List）即可囉！

字彙 應用搶先看：E-mail 會這麼寫！

1. We would like to schedule a <u>conference call</u> in order to discuss the sales in 2016 year and the coming year. Could you please let me know if the following date / time works for you?

   我們想安排個<u>電話會議</u>，好跟您討論 2016 年和明年銷售的事，請問下列哪個日期／時間您比較方便呢？

2. Our teleconference number is +1 (858) 925-1202. When prompted, enter access code 1234# to join the conference.

   我們的電話會議號碼為 +1 (858) 925-1202，聽到語音提示後，請按授權碼 1234#，就可以加入會議了。

3. I could use Skype for our conference call and share my screen with you. We are "immuno.science". Please add me to your Contacts List.

   我可以用 Skype 來開我們的電話會議，也可將我的螢幕畫面分享給你。我們公司的帳戶名是「immuno.science」，請把我加入你的聯絡人清單中。

Part 6 ─ 業務與行銷

 字彙 應用開口說：電話要這麼講！ Track 107

M ▶ Manufacturer 廠商　　D ▶ Distributor 代理商

M ▶ Hi, I have planned two days for my Taiwan visit. I am looking at the week of the 16th of October and probably the 18th and 19th tentatively. Are you available to meet me then?

廠商 ▶ 嗨，我打算安排個兩天到台灣，時間應會在 10 月 16 號那個星期，暫定 18 號和19 號，您那時有空嗎？

D ▶ I'm glad to hear that you're coming to Taiwan! Let me check my schedule... Yes! I can arrange to meet you then!

代理商 ▶ 很高興聽到您要來台的消息！讓我查一下我的行程……，可以！我那時可安排跟您碰面！

M ▶ Great! I will let you know more info when I have a final version of my business trip itinerary. By the way, which hotel do you recommend I stay in Taipei?

廠商 ▶ 太好了！等我行程完全確認後，我就會把更多的訊息告訴您。對了，請問您推薦我住在台北的哪間飯店呢？

D ▶ You could stay in the Grand Hyatt Taipei. It's near our office.

代理商 ▶ 您可以住在台北君悅酒店，它就在我們公司附近。

M ▶ Okay. I'll book that hotel as you suggested. One more thing. Could you arrange a pick-up for me at the airport?

廠商 ▶ 好的，我會依您的建議訂在這家酒店。還有一件事，您可以幫我安排接機嗎？

D ▶ Sure! No problem!

代理商 ▶ 當然！沒問題！

Part 6｜業務與行銷

字字 計較說分明

access [ˈæksɛs] *v.* 進入、進入的權利、（電腦）存取

例 In order to access the conference call, all participants should dial: +1 855 093 2007.

要進入參加電話會議，所有的與會者都請撥打＋1 855 093 2007。

---

accommodation [əˌkɑməˈdeʃən] *n.* 住宿、預計房間（或座位）

例 We can arrange accommodation for you either at the conference venue itself or somewhere close by.

我們可以為您安排住宿，住在會議舉行的這個地方或附近。

---

itinerary [aɪˈtɪnəˌrɛrɪ] *n.* 旅行計畫、旅程、路線

例 The final itinerary and other important information about the conference will be sent to you in due course.

這場會議的確定行程與其他重要資訊到時候會再發給您。

---

prompt [prɑmpt] *v.* 提示、提詞

例 When you're prompted, enter the six-digit conference ID, followed by hash (#).

當提示訊息出現後，請按六碼的會議識別碼，打完後按井字

鍵（＃）。

....

teleconference [`tɛləˌkɑnfərəns]   *n.*   電話會議
= teleconferencing

例 Are you available on any of the following days at 8am Taiwan (5pm San Diego) for our next teleconference?

您下列哪一天的台灣時間上午 8 點（聖地牙哥下午 5 點）時，有空開我們下一場的電話會議呢？

....

tentative [`tɛntətɪv]   *adj.*   暫時的

例 We are pleased to announce that our 2017 Distributor Meeting will take place on March 6-8, 2017 and our tentative schedule is as follows.

我們很高興要來通知您，2017 年代理商會議將於 2017 年 3 月 6～8 日舉行，我們暫定的行程如下所示。

Part 6 ── 業務與行銷

6-3 業績檢討
Sales Meeting

The revenue has risen by x %...

字彙 導覽解說

　　在業務檢討會議上劈頭就談的大事通常就是業績啦！要檢討業績，當然先要將現況實績攤在陽光下，曝光了之後，當然也不能輕輕放過，一定要繼續分析比較，跟前期比、跟去年同期比、跟目標比、跟競爭者比，另外也要抓價格來談，看看價格影響業績的狀況……，有比較就一定會看出增減，所以我們在這就來瞧瞧可以怎麼論過往的高低囉！

1. 拍手慶「升」！- 有增加喔：rose / increased / climbed / grew / mounted up / went up；增加很多喔：hiked / shoot up / soared / skyrocketed / surged / boomed

2. 「降」怎麼行？- 怎麼減少了：decreased / reduced / fell / dropped / declined / went down /dipped；-怎麼掉那麼多：slumped / plummeted / plunged / nosedived / tumbled

3. 「平」心而論！- remained steady / remained constant / remained stable / stayed constant / were flat-lining / leveled out / leveled off / stabilized

4. 高高低低沒個準： fluctuated / rose and fell

📧 字彙 應用搶先看：E-mail 會這麼寫！

1. We're glad to see that <u>the revenue</u> from new product sales <u>has risen by almost 60%</u> compared with this time last year.
   我們很高興看到新產品<u>銷售業績</u>比起去年此時<u>上升了將近 60%</u>。

2. The data shows that the number of your sales has dropped significantly compared to the figures last year.
   資料顯示您們的銷售額比起去年下降得非常多。

3. In the latest quarter, our A101 series sales has continued to grow at a similar rate, while B202 series sales has dropped slightly but still is growing at 2.4%.
   在最近這一季，我們 A101 系列產品的銷售額的成長速度與先前差不多，但 B202 系列銷售額的成長率就有些下降，但還是有成長，比率為 2.4%。

字彙 應用開口說：電話要這麼講！ Track 110

M ▶ Manufacturer 廠商   **D** ▶ Distributor 代理商

M ▶ We noticed that the amount of your orders in June dropped by about 40%! Is there any reason why sales plummeted?

廠商▶ 我們注意到您們六月的訂單金額掉了大概有40%！請問這銷售額大幅降低是有什麼特別的原因嗎？

D ▶ Yes, we lost 2 major projects last month... Do you remember we told you previously that our competitor, Summit, offered extremely low prices in the market?

代理商▶ 有的，我們上個月輸掉了兩個重要的案子⋯⋯，您還記得我們先前告訴過您「高峰」這家競爭者在市場上報超低的價格嗎？

M ▶ Yes, I do remember. But were these 2 projects both lost to Summit?

廠商▶ 是的，我還記得，但是這兩個案子都是輸給「高峰」嗎？

D ▶ Yes...

代理商▶ 是的⋯⋯。

M ▶ We mustn't lose more

廠商▶ 之後的訂單我們不應

orders! For future projects, please do give us any competitor information in advance regarding the prices you're up against. We'll offer our support as much as possible.

該再輸了！往後的案子請務必事先給我們任何您們跟競爭者競價的價格資訊，我們會盡可能地提供支援給您們。

D ▶ It's great to hear that! We'll make every effort to manage projects more efficiently!

代理商 ▶ 聽到您這樣說真好！我們會盡一切的努力讓我們能更有效率地掌握案子！

字字 計較說分明

 Track 111

fluctuate [`flʌktʃʊˌet］ *v.* 波動、變動

例 The online sales growth rate has fluctuated around the 4 % to 5 % range.

線上銷售的成長率在 4%到 5%的區間範圍內上下波動。

相關字 fluctuation [ˌflʌktʃʊˋeʃən] *n.*

---

increase [ɪnˋkris］ *v.* 增加、增大、增強

例 As a new brand in the market, there is a need to continue to expand and increase our visibility.

我們是市場上的新品牌，得要持續擴充與增加我們的能見度。

相關字 increase [ˋɪnkris] *n.* （名詞的重音在第一音節喔！）

---

plunge [plʌndʒ] *v.* 下降、急降

例 Our sales plunged by more than 40 percent during 2015 to their lowest level since 1995.

我們的銷售額在 2015 年驟降的幅度超過了 40%，創 1995 年以來的最低點。

其他字義 俯衝、使投入、使陷入、跳入

---

plummet [`plʌmɪt] *v.* 筆直落下

例 Sales of our tablets have plummeted as customers stick with their current models longer than the typical lifespan of a mobile phone.

我們平板電腦的業績直直落，因為客戶還是繼續使用他們現有的機型，使用的時間比手機的一般壽命還長。

其他字義 *n.* 墜子、測鉛、重壓

skyrocket [`skaɪˌrɑkɪt] *v.* 猛漲、突然高升

例 Our sales have particularly skyrocketed this year, increasing by 40% since January, partly due to a significant upturn in the market.

我們的銷售額今年飆升得特別多，從一月以來提升了 40%，部分原因是因為市場景氣好轉了許多。

surge [sɝdʒ] *v.* 猛漲、激增

例 Our e-commerce sales surged 30 percent over the Christmas holidays.

我們電子商務的銷售額在聖誕節假期期間內激增了百分之三十。

Part 6 業務與行銷

6-4 展覽 Exhibition

If you plan on attending the Annual Meeting...

字彙 導覽解說　　　　　　　　　　　Track 112

　　廠商或代理商參展都是行銷大事，是擴展品牌知名度、提振業績的大好契機！展覽的類型很多，有的叫會議，有的稱展覽，有的是要集思廣益、一起討論。另外，花錢參展不是漂漂亮亮地擺攤擺個幾天就沒事，它的目的列出來可也有個好幾條呢！我們這就來一起紙上看展，也看看展覽背後宏大的目標囉！

1. 展覽名稱大賞：
　　— 都屬會議：Meeting（會議）、Conference（會議）、Congress（代表大會）、Convention（會議、大會）、Colloquium（學習報告會）、Assembly（集會）
　　— 都是展覽：Exhibition（展覽）、Exposition（博覽會）、Fair（展覽）、Show（秀、展覽）、Trade Show（貿易展）
　　— 都算討論會：Seminar（專題討論會）、Symposium（討論會、座談會）、Workshop（專題討論會，研討會）、Panel（討論會）、Forum（論壇）

2. 參展成效大彙整：

— 找出有望客戶（reach potential customers、generate sales leads）

— 直接成交（make direct sales）

— 建立聯絡資料庫（build a contact database）、擴大客戶基礎（expand customer base）

— 建立品牌（brand building）、增加品牌知名度（brand awareness）與品牌能見度（brand visibility）

— 測試市場反應（market test）

📧 字彙 應用搶先看：E-mail 會這麼寫！

1. Please send confirmation if you plan on attending the 58th ASH[1] Annual Meeting & Exposition, 2017 ASCB[2] Annual Meeting, or any upcoming conference held in the US. We plan to coordinate a short distributor meetup at our booth for the major exhibitions.

請跟我們確認是否您有打算參加第 58 屆 ASH 年會暨博覽會、2017 年 ASCB 年會，或是其他將在美國舉行的會議，我們計畫藉著這些主要展覽的舉行，在我們的攤位上安排個簡短的代理商會議。

註[1]：ASH 為 American Society of Hematology，美國血液病學會。

註[2]：ASCB 為 American Society of Cell Biology，美國細胞生物學會。

字彙 應用開口說：電話要這麼講！ Track 113

M ▶ Manufacturer 廠商   D ▶ Distributor 代理商

M ▶ Hi, I'd like to check with you to see if you plan on attending the upcoming ASH Annual Meeting & Exposition?

廠商 ▶ 嗨，我想來問問您有要參加即將舉行的 ASH 年會暨博覽會嗎？

D ▶ Yes! I will be attending ASH this year!

代理商 ▶ 有的！我會參加 ASH 今年的展覽。

M ▶ Great! I will be available to meet with you on Sunday, December 4th. We can meet at 5pm when the exposition closes on that day. Does that sound good to you?

廠商 ▶ 太好了！那我可以排 12 月 4 號星期天跟您見面，我們可以約那天博覽會結束後的下午 5 點碰面，好嗎？

D ▶ Yeah, then I could have more time to share with you the business and marketing status in Taiwan!

代理商 ▶ 好啊，這樣我就有多一點的時間可以跟您分享一下台灣的業務跟市場狀況了。

M ▶ That's what I wanted to know more about! Excellent! By the way, please note, our booth number is 202.

廠商 ▶ 那就是我想知道的呢！太棒了！對了，請記一下，我們的攤位號碼是202。

D ▶ Got it!

代理商 ▶ 好的！

M ▶ And after the meeting, we can go to dinner together!

廠商 ▶ 那開完會之後，我們就可以一起去吃晚餐囉！

D ▶ I love that arrangement! Ha-ha...

代理商 ▶ 這樣的安排我喜歡！哈哈……。

Part 6 ｜業務與行銷

 Track 114

字字 計較說分明

exhibition [ˌɛksə`bɪʃən] *n.* 展覽，展示會

例 Please accept our invitation to attend the exhibition opening which will take place in the hall on the 25th of September.

請接受我們的邀請，前來參加 9 月 25 日在大廳舉行的展覽開幕式。

---

exposition [ˌɛkspə`zɪʃən] *n.* 博覽會、展覽會

例 Please provide me the link to the exposition enabling us to review its related topics.

請給我這個博覽會的網站連結，好讓我們能看一下有什麼相關的主題。

---

lead [lid] *n.* 線索、有望客戶名單、指導

例 Please follow up with the attached leads we've acquired from the 2016 ASCB[3] Annual Meeting that was held last week.

我們上星期在 ASCB 2016 年年會上取得了有望客戶名單如附，還請連絡處理。

其他字義 *v.* 引導、通向； *n.* lead *[lɛd]* 鉛

註[3]：ASCB 為 American Society of Cell Biology，美國細胞生物學會。

seminar [ˈsɛməˌnɑr]　*n.*　研討會

例 I'd like to inform you that we are going to give a seminar in the upcoming conference. 在此通知您一聲，我們在即將舉行的會議中，將會辦一場研討會。

其他字義 （大學）專題討論課；搭配詞 Joint Seminar 聯合研討會

---

visibility [ˌvɪzəˈbɪlətɪ]　*n.*　能見度

例 The primary purpose of marketing the online business is to promote our service and to increase our website visibility.

行銷我們線上業務的主要目的在於推廣我們的服務，並增加我們網站的能見度。

---

workshop [ˈwɜkˌʃɑp]　*n.*　專題討論會，研討會、工作坊、研習坊

例 We will customize a workshop especially for you and focus on your application or specific needs.

我們會專門為您設計個專題研討會，以針對您的應用與特定需求。

Part 6 業務與行銷

6-5 參展準備
Exhibition Preparation

We'll provide catalogs for you to distribute at...

 Track 115

　　公司參展，茲事體大！而大事就該大肆準備、事先規劃，才能讓該到位的都在參展前都到位！廠商參展，會邀代理商與客戶前往，而代理商參展，就會請求廠商支援，提供海報、文宣、展期特價折扣與贈品等，同時廠商也會想要瞭解代理商的促銷規畫等等。參展前的準備工作不少，我們這就來探個究竟囉！

1. **展覽重點要知**：廠商會要瞭解展覽的議程（program）與主題（topics），會請代理商提供網頁連結（link），以能有個通透的瞭解。

2. **書面資料要到**：展覽上會要展示海報（posters），以及發送單張型錄（flyers）、型錄（catalogs）或印刷文宣（literature）等資料。

3. **折扣放送要有**：展場上要刺激買氣，折扣放送一定不能少！有的公司會給折扣券（coupon），有的會訂出特價折扣

（special discount）來吸引客戶在展場上或展期內下單。

4. **促銷好禮要備齊**：促銷禮品（promotional gifts）的設計與組合鐵定是參展籌畫的重點！展場上祭出的小禮物一般分為人人有獎的贈品（giveaways），以及參與活動所拿的好康獎品（prizes）囉！

字彙 應用搶先看：E-mail 會這麼寫！

1. Please send me the link to the conference so that we could review its program to decide what the appropriate literature and catalogs are.

請給我這個會議的網頁連結，這樣我們就可看一下它的議程，好決定這個展覽適合哪些印刷文宣和型錄。

2. We would be happy to provide updated literature, catalogs, and a few promotional gift items for you to distribute at the upcoming Conference. Let me know the date by which you would like to receive all of these items so that we can plan accordingly.

我們很樂意提供給新的文宣資料與型錄，還有一些促銷禮品，讓您們在即將到來的會議中發送。請告訴我您想要在哪一天收到所有這些品項，這樣我們就可依您要求來安排。

字彙 應用開口說：電話要這麼講！ Track 116

D ▶ Distributor 代理商　M ▶ Manufacturer 廠商

D ▶ Hi, I'd like to check with you whether you have made a decision regarding the special discount that you could offer for the upcoming exhibition.

代理商▶ 嗨，我想問一下對於即將舉行的展覽，您已經決定能給的特別折扣有多少了嗎？

M ▶ I just spoke with our Manager and we have agreed to create a special promotion for you in which we will offer you an additional 15% discount on Set products.

廠商▶ 我才剛跟我們經理談了這事，我們同意提供給您一個特別促銷方案，針對套組產品我們可給您再多 15％的額外折扣。

D ▶ Thanks a lot for your support!

代理商▶ 謝謝您的支持！

M ▶ It will be applied from the date of the exhibition until April 30, 2017.

廠商▶ 這項折扣從展覽第一天開始適用，到2017 年 4 月 30 日結束。

D ▶ Great! This will allow us to better promote Set products at the exhibition.

M ▶ The discount can be offered at your discretion, but please disclose the discount you plan to offer to your customers prior to the start of the sale!

代理商 ▶ 太棒了！這可讓我們在展覽中對套組產品推廣得更好。

廠商 ▶ 這折扣就看您自己怎麼使用了，不過得要在促銷開始前就將您打算要推的折扣優惠告訴客戶！

Part 6 業務與行銷

字字 計較說分明

attendee [əˋtɛndi]　*n.*　出席者

例 Below is a list of literature that we recommend would be of interest to attendees at this conference.

我們建議的印刷文宣資料清單如下，這些資料參觀的人應會有興趣。

---

coupon [ˋkupɑn]　*n.*　減價優待券

例 In addition to the usual marketing materials, I can provide you with a 10% discount coupon for one purchase of our products.

除了一般的行銷素材品項之外，我還可以提供給您購買我們產品可享一次的 10%折扣券優惠。

---

giveaways [ˋgɪvəˌwe]　*n.*　贈品

例 Giving away promotional gifts, like pens, key rings these giveaways, with our company logo or name written upon it will create a long lasting presence in the memory of the customers.

分送印著我們商標或公司名的促銷禮品，像是筆、鑰匙圈的這些贈品，可以讓客戶將我們記得久些。

poster [`postɚ]　*n.*　海報

例 How are you going to present our brand in this conference? Which posters are to be shown on the booth wall?

您會在會展上怎麼樣展現我們的品牌呢？在攤位的牆上會貼出哪些海報呢？

program [`progræm]　*n.*　程序、方案、計畫

例 Please check the conference program for the details on the time and date of speeches.

請看會議議程的資料，裡頭有演講的日期與時間這些明細。

traffic [`træfɪk]　*n.*　流量、運輸、運載量

例 We should think of some exhibition attractions to increase the traffic to our exhibition stand.

我們應該想一些會場上的吸睛焦點，這樣才能增加我們攤位的來客量。

其他字義 交通、買賣、交往

Part 6 業務與行銷

6-6 促銷活動
Promotional Campaign
We're offering a **promotion** to our distributors...

　　促銷一定要有好康，有效的促銷一定要有讓客戶實在忍不住買來試試、一不小心就放肆多買一些的衝動啊！促銷手法實在很多，促銷口號叫出來都很聳動，但聳動的背後可還有好些但書限制呢！我們來且看且走，瞭解一下促銷活動的放送說明與一般的限制條件囉！

1. **有值有量有多賺**：促銷方式反應在價上就會有折扣優惠，像是定價（list price）打個八折（20% off discount），或是像訂單總額超過（Order more than）US$ 1,000 即可享 US$ 100 折價的滿額優惠。若是反應在量上，就有像是買一送一（Buy 1 get 1 free）或買大送小的優惠囉！

2. **吾生也有涯，促銷亦必有終時**：看到優惠時眼睛會一亮，但也請一路亮下去，看完整份促銷通知，看特惠是到何時終了（Offer ends on... Offer valid until... Offer is valid until...

One week only...）！

3. **限制一定在：**促銷活動的設計一定會有限定條件（limits），限區域（regions or countries）、限使用次數，如一個客戶限用一次（one time use only per customer），以及優惠不得併用（combine）等等，符合就贏得好康，不符就謝謝再連絡囉！

📧 字彙 應用搶先看：E-mail 會這麼寫！

1. We're glad to inform you that <u>we're offering a promotion to our distributors</u> from April 1st to June 30th. Any customer who buys from our variety of products at a total of more than $ 2,500 will get 25% discount on his / her next order. 很高興地要在此通知您，<u>我們將要推出一項促銷方案給我們的代理商</u>，期間將自 4 月 1 日開始，至 6 月 30 日結束。任何客戶購買我們的各項產品，只要總金額超過$ 2,500，就可享有 25%的折扣，可在下次訂單中扣抵。

Part 6 業務與行銷

249

字彙 應用開口說：電話要這麼講！ Track 119

D ▶ Distributor 代理商　　**M** ▶ Manufacturer 廠商

D ▶ Hi, I see from your latest Newsletter that you'll run a promotional campaign next month. If we order more than $3,000, a discount of 25% will be granted, right?

代理商 ▶ 嗨，我看到您最新的電子報裡頭說下個月會有促銷活動，若是訂滿 $3,000，就可享 25％的折扣，對嗎？

M ▶ Yes, that's correct!

廠商 ▶ 是的，沒錯！

D ▶ That's great! The discount is even larger than our distributor discount. We can place more orders with you next month and benefit from it!

代理商 ▶ 太棒了！這折扣比我們的代理商折扣還大，我們下個月可以多下幾個訂單，多多利用這個好康呢！

M ▶ Wait a moment... Do you know the restrictions of the campaign?

廠商 ▶ 等一下……，您知道這個活動的限制嗎？

D ▶ No... What are they?

代理商 ▶ 不知耶……，是什麼限制呢？

M ▶ They're written at the bottom of the Newsletter. Customers are allowed to use the discount once during the promotion period. But you still can get good use out of it by placing a large order to utilize this special discount!

廠商 ▶ 這些限制條件寫在電子報下方那兒，客戶在促銷期間只能使用一次折扣，不過您還是可好好利用一下，您可以下個大單來使用這個折扣啊！

字字 計較說分明

 Track 120

campaign [kæm`pen]   *n.*   活動

例 Please discuss with us the promotional campaigns that you're going to run throughout this year, so we can know how to best help you.

請跟我們討論一下您們今年一整年想推出的促銷活動,這樣我們也可以知道能怎麼來協助您們。

---

combine [kəm`baɪn]   *v.*   結合、聯合

例 Please note that the special discount cannot be combined with any other discounts or promotions.

請注意,這個特價折扣不能與其他折扣或促銷方案併用。

相關字 combination [ˌkɑmbə`neʃən]   *n.*

---

duration [djʊ`reʃən]   *n.*   持續期間

例 We devised an extensive promotion duration from Sep. 1st to Nov. 30th, 2016 to allow customers to make the best use of it!

我們設計了一個頗長的促銷期,從 2016 年九月一日開始,到十一月三十日結束,好讓客戶們能夠好好利用呢!

相關字 durable [`djʊrəbl̩] *adj.* 耐用的、持久的;durability [ˌdjʊrə`bɪlətɪ]   *n.*   耐久性

limit [`lɪmɪt]　*v.*　*n.*　限制

例 As a limited time offer, we are currently running the promotional campaign of "Buy 2 Get 1 Free on Selected Items"!

我們推出限時特惠，為您送上「精選品項，買二送一」的促銷方案！

相關字 limitation [ˌlɪməˋteʃən]　*n.*

promotion [prəˋmoʃən]　*n.*　促銷

例 This promotion is open to end users placing orders online.

此促銷適用於最終使用者在線上所下的訂單。

qualify [`kwɑləˌfaɪ]　*v.*　具備合格條件

例 This offer will apply to all qualifying orders received between April 1 – June 30, 2017.

在 2017 年四月一日至六月三十日期間內所有合乎條件的訂單，都可適用此特惠。

相關字 qualification [ˌkwɑləfəˋkeʃən]　*n.*　資格、資格證書

7-1 訓練課程
Training Courses

We recommend you join us for the sales training...

　　廠商舉行的訓練課程類別名稱差不多會有這些個：業務訓練（Sales Training）、技術訓練（Technical Training）、代理商訓練（Distributor Training）、代理商業務訓練（Distributor Sales Training）、產品訓練（Product Training）等等，這些訓練並非個個單獨分立，而是你泥中有我、我泥中有你那樣地互有交集。我們在這兒就挑個鮮明的兩大類來說說囉！

1. **業務訓練：**廠商舉行業務訓練，有時也就是稱為代理商訓練，廠商多也會要求代理商提出簡報（presentation）。訓練內容多是包括市場分析（marketing analysis）、目標客群（target customer base）、行銷策略（marketing strategies）、產品介紹（product briefing）等等。

2. **技術訓練：**技術訓練對產品的剖析（product analysis）可就不客氣啦！從產品的介紹、概要（overview）說明，到應用

（application）、操作（operation）、問題解決（troubleshooting）等等，一定要說個明白、講個透徹，才算是真技術訓練呢！

字彙 應用搶先看：E-mail 會這麼寫！

1. <u>We</u> highly <u>recommend that you join us for this sales training.</u> The agenda for the training will include Top 10 Products, New Products, Opportunity and Challenges, Marketing Strategies and Tips & Tricks for Sales force, etc.

<u>我們</u>強烈<u>建議您前來參加這場銷售訓練</u>，安排的流程內容將會包括十大熱銷產品、新產品、機會與挑戰、行銷策略，以及給業務人員的提示與技巧等等。

2. As we offer a wide range of product lines for various research areas, we will hold monthly product training sessions to help your team become more familiar with our products including their application and operation.

由於我們產品線的涵蓋很廣，供應給各種不同研究領域使用，因此我們將會舉行每個月的產品訓練課程，以讓您的團隊對我們的產品更熟悉，也能更瞭解產品的應用與操作。

字彙 應用開口說：電話要這麼講！ Track 122

D ▶ Distributor 代理商　M ▶ Manufacturer 廠商

D ▶ Hello, I'm glad to tell you that we've won the tender!

代理商 ▶ 哈囉，我很高興要來跟您說件事，我們得標了！

M ▶ Congratulations!

廠商 ▶ 恭喜！

D ▶ Thanks for your support on the pricing!

代理商 ▶ 謝謝您在價格上的協助！

M ▶ We can support you further to ensure successful usage of the products you are about to supply. Would you like to have training?

廠商 ▶ 我們可以再給您更多的協助，確保對於您將要供應的產品可以使用成功，您想要受個訓練嗎？

D ▶ Yeah, that'll be great!

代理商 ▶ 好啊，那會很不錯！

M ▶ Okay! So we'll provide

廠商 ▶ 好的！那我們就會排

technical training for you better understand the operation and also new developments in our product lines.

個技術訓練給您，讓您對操作、對我們的產品線的發展都能多多瞭解。

D ▶ That'll be helpful! Thank you!

代理商 ▶ 那會很有幫助，謝謝！

M ▶ We really do look forward to continuing to enhance our relationship, and that's actually why I believe that training will benefit both of us!

廠商 ▶ 我們真的期望能繼續合作並更加強彼此的關係，也正是因為如此，我認為訓練會對我們雙方都有好處！

D ▶ Yes, I think a technical training will help us ensure that customers will enjoy the full advantages of your products!

代理商 ▶ 是啊，我認為技術訓練可以幫助我們，讓我們確保客戶能夠感受到您產品的所有優點！

 Track 123

analysis [ə`næləsɪs] *n.* 分析、解析

例 Through product analysis, we'll understand how well the product does its job compared with other similar products.

透過產品分析，我們就會瞭解這項產品跟其他相似產品比起來有多好。

相關字 analyze [`ænl͵aɪz] *v.*

---

briefing [`brifɪŋ] *n.* 簡報

例 This short online briefing will give you all the basic information you need to understand the product.

這份線上的簡短簡報可提供您要瞭解這項產品所需的所有基本資訊。

---

course [kors] *n.* 課程

例 The course fee will include all training, course materials, food and accommodation, usually from the evening of the first date to the afternoon of the last date.

課程費用將會包括所有的訓練、課程材料，以及從第一天傍晚到最後一天下午的食宿。

presentation [ˌprizɛn`teʃən] *n.* 簡報

例 We will surely let you know, in advance, if we will need a presentation from you in the Meeting.

若我們需要您在會議中提出簡報，我們一定會事先告訴您。

其他字義 贈送、授予、提出、呈現、演出

相關字 present *[prɪ`zɛnt]* *v.* ；present *[`prɛznt]* *n.* 禮物； *adj.* 出席的、現在的；presence *[`prɛzns]* *n.* 出席、風度、風範

---

session [`sɛʃən] *n.* 課程、講習班、會議、集會

例 We will be introducing our new technology and products in our first session.

在第一個課程裡，我們會介紹我們的新技術與新產品。

---

slide [slaɪd] *n.* 投影片、幻燈片

例 We have uploaded the presentation slides on Egnyte for your use and reference before the training.

我們已將簡報投影片上載到 Egnyte 雲端伺服器上了，您在訓練開始前可開來看看並參考。

其他字義 滑動、山崩

7-2 線上研討會 Webinar

Our product training **webinar** will be hosted on...

 Track 124

　　古早時代一定得聚首才辦得了的訓練課程或研討會，在這年頭很多都已轉為線上研討會（webinar）了。線上研討會舉行的程序跟傳統差不多，但多了些線上專屬的做法與功能，我們這就來瞧瞧囉！

1. **報上名來**：要上課就請先登記（register），因線上研討會通常會給定幾個日期與時間任君選擇，所以也請選個場次。在登記完成後，就請等著廠商發來確認（Confirmation）或邀請（Invitation）囉！

2. **如何使得**：要在線上上課，還有些必要條件（prerequisite），如要用電腦來上課，就會要從廠商發來的邀請點入，輸入會議識別碼（Meeting ID）與參加者識別碼（Participant ID），若要用電話上課，就會告訴你要按（press）何鍵來加入囉！

3. **務必回報：**上完課後多半要做個調查（take a survey），填完才算完成課程！

4. **往事還能回味：**線上研討會都會有錄影錄音（recorded file、recording）的存證資料，讓上過課的人回味，讓錯過的人也能體會！

✉ 字彙 應用搶先看：E-mail 會這麼寫！

1. We are happy to inform you that <u>our</u> first monthly <u>product</u> <u>training</u> <u>webinar</u> <u>will be hosted on</u> Oct. 17th! Please register for the date and time that works best for you!

很高興要來通知您，<u>我們</u>第一場的每月<u>產品訓練線上研討會就要在十月十七日舉行了！</u>請登記個對您最方便的日期與時間！

2. Each webinar has a unique 9, 10, or 11-digit number called a Meeting ID that will be required to join a Zoom meeting. If you are joining via telephone, you will need the teleconferencing number provided in the invitation.

每一場線上研討會都有個獨特的 9、10 或 11 碼號碼，稱為會議識別碼，要加入 Zoom 視訊會議，就需要此號碼。若您是要透過電話加入，您就需要輸入邀請函所提供的電話會議號碼。

字彙 應用開口說：電話要這麼講！ Track 125

D ▶ Distributor 代理商　　**M** ▶ Manufacturer 廠商

D ▶ I've registered to join the upcoming webinar, but I'm not sure how to join the meeting exactly. Could you tell me how to do it?

代理商 ▶ 我已經登記了要參加即將舉行的線上研討會，但我不確定到底要怎麼加入開會，您可以告訴我要怎麼做嗎？

M ▶ Sure! In fact, I do have a short tutorial film for your reference. I can e-mail the link to you.

廠商 ▶ 沒問題！事實上，我就有一份教學短片可給您參考，我可以e-mail 影片的連結給您。

D ▶ Great! Thank you! By the way, can you tell me how long the webinar will take?

代理商 ▶ 太棒了！謝謝您！對了，您能不能告訴我這場線上研討會會開多久呢？

M ▶ It should take around 1-2 hours depending on how many questions you ask and what discussions stem from the

廠商 ▶ 應該會開個 1～2 個小時左右，要看您們問的問題多不多，還要看從訓練衍生出什麼樣的討論。

training.

D ▶ I see.

M ▶ Oh! I'd like to remind you of one thing. You will be prompted to take a survey at the end of the webinar. Please fill out the survey, as it will help us to better understand and assist you in future training!

代理商▶ 瞭解。

廠商▶ 喔！我要提醒您一件事，在線上研討會最後，會有份調查表請您做一做，那就請您填寫了，這樣可讓我們對您未來的訓練需求更瞭解，也就更能協助您。

字字 計較說分明

 Track 126

invitation [ˌɪnvəˈteʃən] *n.* 邀請、邀請函

例 Web Seminar Invitation: March Distributor Training Webinar. We invite you to attend a web seminar using WebEx. Please note this event requires registration.

網路研討會邀請：三月代理商訓練線上研討會。我們邀請您使用 WebEx 來參加網路研討會，請注意此活動須事先登記。

---

participant [pɑrˈtɪsəpənt] *n.* 參與者

例 The hands-on-training is limited to only 10 participants and we will give priority to distributors from overseas.

這一場實作訓練課程僅限 10 人參加，我們會開放讓海外代理商優先報名。

其他字義 participate *[parˈtɪsəˌpet]* *v.* 參加

---

prerequisite [ˌpriˈrɛkwəzɪt] *n.* 必要條件、前提

例 One of the prerequisite skills for this training is that all our training sessions require you to have at least basic computer skills.

參加這個訓練的必備技能之一是所有的訓練課程都至少要具備基本的電腦技能。

其他字義　　*adj.*　不可缺的、必修的

---

survey [sə`ve]　*n.*　調查、調查報告；　*v.*　調查

例 Please fill out this quick survey. Help us understand more about your research for a chance to win a gift!

請填寫這份簡短的調查表，讓我們能多瞭解些您的研究需求，您也有機會贏得好禮！

---

tutorial [tju`torɪəl]　*n.*　個別指導、教學

例 To further assist our customers, we have produced a series of video tutorials available on our website.

為了能進一步協助我們的客戶，我們已錄製了一系列的教學影片，放在網站供您觀看。

---

webinar [wɛmə͵nɑr]　*n.*　線上研討會

= web + seminar

例 Please note that this webinar is hosted for internal training purposes.

請注意這場線上研討會是為了內部訓練目的而舉辦。

7-3 實體研討會 Seminar

We will **organize** a seminar in the conference...

字彙 導覽解說

Track 127

　　廠商或代理商在展覽期間，也常會籌辦研討會，將廠商的重點產品或技術介紹給客戶。而籌辦實體研討會的事務不少，會說到的字彙可也自有一大群，我們一定要來看個熱鬧啊！

1. **關係人等**：要籌辦，就會說到主辦單位（Organizer、Organized by、Hosted by）、協辦單位（Co-organizer、Co-organized by）、贊助單位（Sponsor、Sponsored by）與主持人（Chair、Chaired by）這幾個關係單位／人囉！

2. **重頭戲**：講座的重頭戲就在於演講了，會說到的角色人物包括有主題講者（keynote speaker）、受邀講者（invited speaker），會提到的訊息與資料包括有主題（topic）、摘要（abstract）、簡報（presentation）與文章（article）。而演講結束，最後一定要排個問答（Q & A）時間，讓與會者盡興提問！

3. **相關通知事項**：像是地點（venue、place、location）、時間（time）、議程（agenda、program）都是必然會通知的訊息喔！

✉ 字彙 應用搶先看：E-mail 會這麼寫！

1. We will be delivering a seminar at the conference focusing on the new product we wish to develop in your market. It'll be a good way of getting in front of prospective clients and hopefully generating new orders as a result of the interests shown!

   我們將會在會議中辦一場研討會，針對我們希望在您市場推廣的新產品來進行討論，這將是面對有望客戶，以及希望就這麼將他們表現的興趣轉為新訂單的好方法！

2. We will organize a seminar in the conference and invite our Product Manager to deliver a keynote speech about our latest technology. Please help us in organizing the seminar and invite your key customers and prospects to the seminar.

   我們將會在會議中辦一場研討會，會邀請我們的產品經理針對我們的新技術發表主題演講，請協助我們主辦，並請邀請您的重要客戶與有望客戶前來參加研討會。

 **字彙** 應用開口說：電話要這麼講！ Track 128

D ▶ Distributor 代理商　　**M** ▶ Manufacturer 廠商

D ▶ Hi, you know that we'll be attending a conference in Summer, right?

代理商 ▶ 嗨，您知道我們夏季時會參加一場會議，是吧？

M ▶ Yes, you did tell us about it!

廠商 ▶ 是的，您先前是有説過！

D ▶ That's right. We're thinking about renting a seminar room at the conference. It should be an effective way to position our business as a specialist in the market and also create face-to-face interactions with our preferred customers.

代理商 ▶ 沒錯，我們在想要不要在會議中租一個研討會會議室，這應該是個建立我們在市場上專業地位，以及製造跟優質客戶面對面交流的好方法。

M ▶ That's a great idea! I totally agree with you! How can we assist you?

廠商 ▶ 很好的想法！我完全同意！我們可以怎樣協助呢？

D ▸ We'd like to invite your Product Specialist to deliver a speech about your newly developed technology. Could you arrange that for us?

代理商 ▸ 我們想要邀請您的產品專員針對您們最新發展的技術來發表一篇演講，請問您可以替我們這樣安排嗎？

M ▸ Sure! Just tell me the date and the time allocated for the speech and I'll then arrange the trip schedule for our Product Specialist!

廠商 ▸ 當然可以！您只要告訴我日期跟演講的時間長度，我就會替我們的產品專員安排出差行程！

D ▸ Thank you so much!

代理商 ▸ 真的非常謝謝您！

字字 計較說分明

Track 129

abstract [`æbstrækt] *n.* 摘要、梗概

例 The deadline for abstract submission is midnight GMT, Friday, April 7th 2017.

摘要的繳交期限為 2017 年格林威治標準時間的四月七日星期五午夜。

article [`ɑrtɪkl] *n.* 文章、物品

例 For more information, click the link to read the full article and see the seminar program.

請點此連結以觀看更多的訊息，裡頭有完整的文章與研討會的議程。

keynote [`ki͵not] *n.* （演說等的）主旨；基調

例 We are delighted to invite Professor Chen as our keynote speaker.

我們很高興能邀請到陳教授來擔任我們的主題講者。

其他字義 （音樂）主音

organize [`ɔrgə͵naɪz] *v.* 組織、安排

例 The hands-on training course is organized by our company, in collaboration with a consulting firm.

這個實用訓練課程是由我們公司主辦，也有跟一間顧問公司合作。

相關字 organizer [`ɔrgəˌnaɪzə] n. 主辦單位

organized [`ɔrgənˌaɪzd] adj. 有條理的

organization [ˌɔrgənəˈzeʃən] n. 組織、機構、體制、結構

搭配詞 a non-governmental organization (NGO) 非政府組織；a non-profit organization (NPO) 非營利組織

---

sponsor [`spansə] v. 贊助； n. 贊助者

例 We will continue to sponsor the charity's events for the next three years.

我們將會在接下來的三年內繼續贊助這一個慈善團體的活動。

---

venue [`vɛnju] n. 集合地、發生地

例 A seminar venue needs to be spacious enough to make each audience feel comfortable and to allow them to keep focused and engaged with the speaker.

研討會的地點場地得要夠寬敞，能讓每位聽眾覺得舒服，也能將注意力集中在講者身上。

8-1 公司簡介
Company Profile

Our company was **established** in yyyy...

字彙 導覽解說

　　廠商與代理商初初相遇時，一定要來一番自我介紹，讓彼此信服對方是可以一起打天下、闖江湖的好夥伴！那介紹時該要有哪些事項來彰顯自己呢？我們這就來介紹一下囉！

1. **從頭說起**：自我介紹要說明公司的概況（profile、overview），通常會從歷史（history）來破題，說源起（origins），說公司的成立（founded、established、incorporated）元年，接著談之後的壯大與成長（growth），再導引到述說今日（today）的輝煌與成就！

2. **說強項說優勢**：請先擱下謙卑、謙卑、再謙卑，一定要說說自己的優勢（strength）！廠商多會強調擁有最先進的（state-of-the-art）技術（technology）與設備（facility），可提供高品質（high quality）的產品；代理商則會強調專業的服務（professional service），會宣揚一下客戶基礎（customer base）有多廣多大！此外，介紹時也可闡述公司的發展（development）、認同的價值（value）、使命

（mission）、願景（vision）或承諾（commitment）等等，讓彼此能有互信互動的基礎與驅力！

📧 字彙 應用搶先看：E-mail 會這麼寫！

1. We develop world-class, cutting-edge chemicals for medical research use. Our mission is to accelerate research by providing the highest quality products, along with superior customer service and technical support.

我們研發世界級、最先進的化學製品供醫學研究使用，我們的使命是要提供最高品質的產品，以及優質的客戶服務與技術支援，以加快研究發展的速度。

2. Our company was established in 1995. Since then we have offered high quality chemicals for research in various fields. We support our customers with a staff of highly experienced professionals as well as a modern, fully-equipped laboratory with capabilities to analyze the majority of the products we offer.

我們公司成立於 1995 年，一直以來都是提供高品質的化學製品，供各個不同領域的研究來使用，我們有極富經驗的專業人員來為我們的客戶提供服務，另外也擁有現代且配備完整的實驗室，以檢驗我們提供的多數產品。

Part 8｜合作／代理關係

字彙 應用開口說：電話要這麼講！ Track 131

M▶ Manufacturer 廠商　　**D▶** Distributor 代理商

M▶ Hi, I received your email asking for a quote. However, as you are not our official distributor, I need to speak with you prior to issuing any quote to you. We need to evaluate the potential opportunity of us working together. Could you tell me about your business?

廠商▶ 嗨，我收到了您要求我們報價的email，但因為您不是我們的正式代理商，我在報價前要跟您談談，好評估一下合作的潛在商機有多少。您能跟我說說您的公司嗎？

D▶ Sure! Our company was founded in 1995. We're the exclusive distributor of ACE Int'l in Taiwan. Because of our many years of experience in providing versatile solutions in technically demanding installations, we are able to offer a professional and reliable

代理商▶ 當然！我們公司是在 1995 年成立的，我們是艾斯國際的在台獨家代理。因為我們在高技術要求的安裝案件這方面有很多年的經驗，能夠提供各種不同的解決方案，因此，我們有辦法從頭到尾提供專業和可信賴的服務。

service from start to finish.

M ▶ It's good to hear that you are highly experienced in this field!

廠商 ▶ 很高興聽到您們在這個領域很有經驗！

D ▶ You can rest assured about our ability and also our business potential!

代理商 ▶ 關於我們的能力和業務潛力，請您放心！

M ▶ Great! We're happy to have this opportunity to cooperate with you. I'll send you our quote later!

廠商 ▶ 太棒了！我們很高興能有這個機會跟您合作，我待會兒就會發報價單給您！

Part 8 ─ 合作／代理關係

275

字字 計較說分明

 Track 132

commit [kə`mɪt] *v.* 使作出保證、使承擔義務

例 We are committed to helping provide you with high quality products and professional service.

我們承諾會協助提供給您高品質的產品與專業的服務。

其他字義 犯（罪）、做（錯事）

相關字 commitment *[kə`mɪtmənt]* *n.* 承諾、保證、託付、委任

---

establish [ə`stæblɪʃ] *v.* 建立、創辦

例 After several years of growth, our company moved to Michigan and established our first laboratory.

在幾年的成長之後，我們公司搬到了密西根，建立了我們的第一間實驗室。

---

mission [`mɪʃən] *n.* 使命、任務

例 Our mission is to always deliver excellence throughout all operations of the business and to achieve the highest levels of customer satisfaction.

我們的使命是要在業務執行的各個面向都能成就卓越，讓客戶擁有最高的滿意度。

overview [`ovəˌvju]　*n.*　概要、概觀

例 This page is designed to give you a general overview of the skills needed to operate the instrument.

這一頁是設計用來讓你對操作此儀器所需技能有個概括的瞭解。

---

profile [`profaɪl]　*n.*　簡介、概況

例 For a review of the current products and services we provide, please see our company profile.

若要看我們目前所提供的產品與服務，請見我們的公司簡介。

其他字義 輪廓、外形、剖面（圖）

---

strength [strɛŋθ]　*n.*　長處、優勢、力量

例 The strength of our company lies in the diversity and expertise of our people.

我們公司的優勢在於人員的多樣性與專業度。

相關用法 SWOT 分析 → Strength（優勢）、Weakness（劣勢）、Opportunity（機會）、Threat（威脅）

8-2 獨家代理
Exclusive Distribution

We authorize XXX as the exclusive **distributor**...

　　廠商需要各地代理商提供在地服務，為其開拓全球市場，而代理商需要取得國外廠商的貨源，為客戶牽成，並開拓自身事業版圖的一片天！代理商要能取得貨源，就要取得廠商的授權，以能銷售廠商的產品，因此，在協定合作關係時，就會牽涉到獨家、非獨家代理的議題。我們在這一個單元就先來瞧瞧談獨家代理會談出哪些字兒囉！

1. **獨家報導**：代理商的終極代理境界就是拿下獨家代理權（exclusive distribution right），成為廠商的獨家代理商（exclusive / sole distributor），建立獨家的合作關係（relationship）。

2. **先決條件**：廠商若要給獨家代理，會有些先決條件，像是代理商就不能也是其主要競爭者（arch rival、main rival、main competitor）的代理商，或是代理商得承諾可達一定的銷售

額（sales revenue）或目標（target）等。

3. **為何要「獨」**：要求獨家代理的最主要目的通常就是為了減少在地多個代理之間的爭奪廝殺（reduce local competition between distributors），如此一來，代理商方能不受干擾地制定行銷策略，對市場有更好的掌控力！

✉ 字彙 應用搶先看：E-mail 會這麼寫！

1. We hereby authorize HonTa Co., located at 10F, No. 10, Double-Tenth Rd., Sanchung Dist., New Taipei City, Taiwan, as the exclusive distributor for BASE products in Taiwan. BASE has provided the exclusive distribution right to HonTa Co. in Taiwan for distributing all BASE products. This letter expires on December 31, 2017 and authorizes HonTa Co. to quote, enter into contracts, government tenders and supply the products on our behalf.

   我們在此授權位於新北市三重區雙十路十號十樓的宏大公司，為貝斯產品的臺灣獨家代理商。貝斯提供臺灣的獨家代理權給宏大公司，讓其經銷所有貝斯的產品。此授權書的效期至 2017 年十二月三十一日為止，授權宏大代表我們提供報價、簽立合約、參與政府標案，以及供應產品。

字彙 應用開口說：電話要這麼講！ Track 134

M ▶ Manufacturer 廠商   D ▶ Distributor 代理商

M ▶ We truly appreciate your efforts and dedication to selling our products. We have been thinking about ways of improving our cooperation and we may have a proposition that is worth considering!

廠商 ▶ 我們真的很感謝您在銷售我們產品上所做的努力，我們有在想怎樣能夠讓我們合作得更好，有一個方案可能還滿適合考慮一下的！

D ▶ That really sparks my interest! What's the proposal?

代理商 ▶ 這可真引起了我的興趣！是什麼提議呢？

M ▶ We are prepared to appoint your company our sole distributor in Taiwan!

廠商 ▶ 我們準備指派您的公司為我們在台灣的獨家代理商！

D ▶ Wow! That's wonderful news! We believe this will work to the advantage of our both companies!

代理商 ▶ 哇！超棒的消息耶！我們相信這對我們雙方都會很有幫助！

M ▶ Yeah! As the sole distributor you could enjoy certain benefits, including considerably reducing local competition between distributors! We believe that an exclusive relationship will lead to achieving better sales results, right?

D ▶ That's for sure! Now we can take better control of our marketing efforts!

廠商 ▶ 是啊！身為我們的獨家代理商，您會享有好些個好處，包括當地代理商之間的競爭就會少掉許多！我們相信獨家代理的關係會帶來更好的銷售業績，對嗎？

代理商 ▶ 那是一定的，因為這樣我們在行銷努力上就能掌控得更好了！

Part 8 | 合作／代理關係

字字 計較說分明

Track 135

agent [`edʒənt]　*n.*　代理商、代理人

例 Unfortunately, we have no agent in Taiwan, but we sell the product ourselves all over the world.

抱歉我們在台灣沒有代理商，我們都是自己銷售此產品到世界各地。

相關字 agency *[`edʒənsɪ]*　*n.*　代理機構

---

authorize [`ɔθə͵raɪz]　*v.*　授權給

例 For your requirement of our products or any information, we suggest you contact our authorized agent.

若您有需要我們的產品或任何的訊息，建議您與我們授權的代理商聯絡。

相關字 authorization *[͵ɔθərə`zeʃən]*　*n.*　授權

---

distributor [dɪ`strɪbjətɚ]　*n.*　代理商、代理商

例 We'd like to know whether you could appoint us as your exclusive distributor in Taiwan.

我們想知道是否您可任命我們為您在台灣的獨家代理商。

相關字 distributorship *[dɪ`strɪbjətɚʃɪp]*　*n.*　代理權、銷售權

---

exclusive [ɪk`sklusɪv]　*adj.*　獨家的

例 The exclusive relationship has to be accompanied by some essential preconditions and actions.

獨家關係得要同時搭配一些根本的先決條件與做法。

relationship [rɪ`leʃən`ʃɪp]　*n.*　關係、關聯

例 I really do look forward to continuing and enhancing this relationship with your company.

我真的期待能夠繼續並加強與您公司的關係。

相關字 relation *[rɪ`leʃən]*　*n.*　關係、關聯

represent [ˌrɛprɪ`zɛnt]　*v.*　代理、代表

例 You are authorized to represent our company, quote and sell our products within Taiwan.

我們授權您在台灣代表我公司、提供報價並銷售我們的產品。

相關字 representative *[rɛprɪ`zɛntətɪv]*　*adj.*　代理的、代表的；　*n.*　代表、代理人

Part 8 ｜ 合作／代理關係

8-3 非獨家代理
Non-exclusive Distribution

Our policy is not to give exclusivity...

字彙 導覽解說

　　代理商都會想要廠商給予獨家代理的至高授權，但廠商比較想給的多半是非獨家代理權（non-exclusive distribution right），所以雙方在協商時，代理商會努力想要說服，但廠商也會不斷重申立場，我們就來看看只能給非獨家代理的理由囉！

1. **公司政策（policy）**：有些廠商一點兒也不囉嗦，直接在政策面就規定了只給非獨家代理權！而有的廠商則規定若要求獨家，則須承諾做到一個業績目標值（sales target）！

2. **均分天下**：若廠商看在地的幾家代理商的表現相當，並沒有誰比誰優越（superiority），市場與客群的涵蓋（coverage）程度也差不多，那麼廠商也就不會有意願給任一家獨家代理了。

3. **產品種類多**：有的廠商的產品線（product lines）多且廣，

非單獨一家代理商有辦法對每一種類型的產品都能全力經銷，因而廠商也就不會統而給予獨家代理權。

字彙 應用搶先看：E-mail 會這麼寫！

1. Our policy is not to give exclusivity. However, we could consider an exclusive arrangement if a minimum order value was agreed upon, e.g. US$ 200,000, whereby any difference in amount ordered and the agreed upon target would be invoiced to you at the end of the year.

   我們公司的政策是不給獨家代理權，不過，若是您同意最低訂單金額的要求，例如 US$ 200,000，而且接受所訂金額與所同意目標的差額可在年底開發票給您，那我們就可考慮獨家代理的安排。

2. For now we don't have any intentions to provide a sole distributorship to any of the Taiwanese distributors. I appreciate the progress that you exhibits with our sales, but the current situation is that none of the distributors exhibit a significant superiority over the other.

   目前我們並沒有意願給任何一家台灣代理商獨家代理權，我很感謝您在銷售我們產品上所展現的成長，但現在的狀況是沒有一家代理商在表現上有明顯優於另一家代理商。

字彙 應用開口說：電話要這麼講！ Track 137

D ▶ Distributor 代理商　M ▶ Manufacturer 廠商

D ▶ Could you appoint us as your exclusive distributor in Taiwan?

代理商 ▶ 您能不能任命我們為您們的在臺獨家代理商呢？

M ▶ Considering that we have several hundred products and it is difficult for one distributor to promote all the products at the same effective and successful level, we prefer not to give exclusivity to any distributor.

廠商 ▶ 考慮到我們有好幾百種的產品，要一家代理商能夠對所有的產品都能以同樣的效率、同樣成功地來推廣，是很難的，所以我們偏好不給任何一家代理商獨家的代理權。

D ▶ I see... How about giving us the exclusivity for your research products? You know that some tenders request that we submit a letter of exclusive authorization.

代理商 ▶ 瞭解……，那若是就您們的研究產品這一類給我們做獨家，如何？您知道有些標案就會要我們提出獨家授權書。

M ▶ We should be able to proceed in that way... If, in any case, a letter of exclusive authorization is needed for single products, we can issue such a letter to you as we know and understand this is important and necessary to secure the business!

廠商 ▶ 我們應該是可以這麼來做……，若是，有任何個別產品有需要獨家授權書的話，我們是可以出具給您的，我們知道這對拿下訂單是重要且必要的條件！

字字 計較說分明

appoint [ə`pɔɪnt]　*v.*　任命、指派

例 Since you has a sufficient business focus on promoting our products, we decided to appoint your company as our sole distributor in your country.

因為您在行銷我們產品這方面夠投入，所以我們決定任命 貴公司為我們在您國家的獨家代理商。

---

approach [ə`protʃ]　*v.*　接近、靠近

例 Some of our products are mainly used in routine testing and giving you exclusivity would block us from approaching this market in Taiwan.

我們有些產品主要用來做常規檢測，而給了您獨家代理權就會讓我們無法接觸到這一塊的臺灣市場。

其他字義　*n.*　接近、方法、通道

---

coverage [`kʌvərɪdʒ]　*n.*　覆蓋範圍

例 The plan envisages a two-stage approach to maximize market and customer coverage.

這個計畫設想的是透過兩階段的作法，將市場與客戶涵蓋範圍擴充到最大程度。

其他字義 保險項目（或範圍）、新聞報導

superiority [səˌpɪrɪˋɔrətɪ] *n.* 優越、優勢

例 If innovation is successful, the superiority of the new product over the existing ones will be reflected in reduced fixed costs.

若是這一項創新是成功的，那麼新產品優於現有產品的表現將會反映在降低固定成本上。

相關字 superior [səˋpɪrɪɚ] *adj.* 較好的、較優的

---

treat [trit] *v.* 對待、看待、把……看作

例 We'll forward sales leads to you and treat you as an exclusive partner – even without a written exclusivity agreement.

我們會將有望客戶資料轉給您，將您視為我們的獨家合作夥伴 — 即使沒有書面的獨家代理權合約。

其他字義 處理、治療、款待

相關字 treatment [ˋtritmənt] *n.* 對待、處理

8-4 購併
Acquisition and Merger

XXX was acquired by XXX.

字彙 導覽解說

　　這些年來廠商購併的這類組織重整大事愈來愈多！對於代理商來説，代理廠牌被購併了真格是大代誌，因為購併別人的廠商多半也有自己的代理商！但若是自家的代理廠商併了別人，那就會想磨刀霍霍，也想要能銷售被併廠牌的產品！現就讓我們來小小捲入組織重整的潮流中，探個究竟吧！

1. **購併啦**：當你收到廠商的來函中寫到「acquire」、「merge」這兩個説購併的字，眼睛都會不自覺地睜大呢！

2. **時程事**：購併事的通知裡頭，一定會將相關的重要時間點／期間説清楚，如正式購併日、購併生效（effective）日、轉換／過渡（transition）期間。

3. **作業方式變動**：改了朝換了代，品牌名（brand）、包裝（packaging）、聯繫人（contacts）、訂單處理（ordering processing）程序都可能會生變！

✉ 字彙 應用搶先看：E-mail 會這麼寫！

1. We would like to follow up with you about the progress we have made over the past month related to the integration of the CORE business into the ACE family. As you may know, CORE was acquired in March, 2016 by ACE, and we have been hard at work to ensure a smooth transition into our facility in Ohio. We are eager to combine ACE's resources with the already successful and innovative product line and staff at CORE.

   要來跟您更新一下過去這幾個月來，我們整合柯爾公司到我們艾思集團的進度。可能您已經知道艾思在 2016 年三月已收購了柯爾公司，我們一直努力地做，為的就是要確保能夠順利將柯爾整合轉換到我們的俄亥俄州廠區。我們現正積極地將艾思的資源與柯爾已經成功推行的創新產品線以及人員結合在一起。

字彙 應用開口說：電話要這麼講！ Track 140

D ▶ Distributor 代理商   M ▶ Manufacturer 廠商

D ▶ I heard about the news that OTTO was recently acquired by your company. Is this correct?

代理商 ▶ 我聽說您們公司最近購併了奧圖公司，是嗎？

M ▶ Yes! We will be announcing the news next week!

廠商 ▶ 是的！我們下星期就會發布這個消息呢！

D ▶ Great to hear that! So we'll be able to sell OTTO products, right?

代理商 ▶ 太棒了！所以我們就可以銷售奧圖的產品了嗎？

M ▶ At this time, our distributors are not authorized to sell the OTTO products. But effective June 1, 2016, Customer Service and Technical Support functions will be formally transitioned to our Ohio location, and you can order their products then.

廠商 ▶ 目前我們的代理商是還不能銷售奧圖的產品，但是從 2016 年六月一日開始，我們將會正式將他們的客服與技術支援作業移轉到我們的俄亥俄廠區，到時候您就可以訂購他們的產品了。

D ▶ Okay, we'll start to promote OTTO products to our customers!

代理商 ▶ 好的，我們會開始推銷奧圖的產品給我們的客戶！

M ▶ We are working to realize additional process efficiencies through our integration efforts and will look to share the benefits of such with our customers!

廠商 ▶ 我們現在正努力整合，以達成額外的製程效率，這樣之後就可以將這些優勢分享給我們的客戶！

Part 8 — 合作／代理關係

293

字字 計較說分明

 Track 141

acquisition [ˌækwə`zɪʃən] *n.* 收購、獲得

例 Since the announcement of our acquisition of CORE, there has been lots of interest to distribute the former CORE products.

自從我們宣布買下了柯爾公司之後，就有許多代理商跟我們表示有興趣經銷先前柯爾的產品。

----

announce [ə`naʊns] *v.* 宣布、發布

例 We are delighted to announce the news that ACE has been granted a patent in the United States for a new technology.

我們很高興要來宣布一個消息，那就是艾思公司的一項新技術已經拿到美國的專利了。

----

integration [ˌɪntə`greʃən] *n.* 整合、完成

例 Integration of these related websites in a unified format helps customers quickly choose the best combination.

將這些相關網站以統一格式整合起來，可讓客戶能更快地選出最好的搭配組合。

----

merger [mɝdʒɚ]　*n.*（公司等的）合併

例 What are the benefits for customers from the merger of ACE and CORE?

對於艾思公司與柯爾公司合併，對客戶的好處是什麼呢？

⋯⋯⋯⋯⋯⋯⋯⋯⋯⋯⋯⋯⋯⋯⋯⋯⋯⋯⋯⋯⋯⋯⋯⋯⋯

streamline [`strim͵laɪn]　*v.*　使有效率、簡化

例 We anticipate that a full conversion of these documents will be completed in the upcoming months and we appreciate your patience as we work to streamline processes.

我們希望這些文件的徹底轉換調整可在接下來的幾個月中完成，也很感謝您在我們努力簡化程序時的耐心相伴。

其他字義　*n.*　流線型；　*v.*　使⋯⋯成流線型

⋯⋯⋯⋯⋯⋯⋯⋯⋯⋯⋯⋯⋯⋯⋯⋯⋯⋯⋯⋯⋯⋯⋯⋯⋯

transition [træn`zɪʃən]　*n.*　轉變、過渡、過渡期

例 We thank you for your time and patience during this transition.

謝謝您在這過渡期間的耐心等候。

8-5 人事異動
Personnel Change

I just wanted to inform you that I'll soon be leaving...

字彙 導覽解說　　　　　　　　　　Track 142

　　廠商組織的變革（organizational change）容易引來大地震，而人事（personnel）上的異動有時也是茲事體大！ 我們在這本書的最後一個單元，就來看看異動的通知內容，也順道來感受、感激、感動一下囉！

1. **為何要離開**：若是你瞄到信件裡有離開（leave）、休假（leave of absence）、追求（pursue）、往前（move forward）這些字眼，請不要懷疑，多半就是接頭的人要換啦！

2. **感傷也感謝**：合作多年的感情，在將要兩散之際，一定會有感傷（sadness），會有一路走來的感激（appreciation），也會表達出共事的榮幸（honor）與愉悦（pleasure）！

3. **祝福**：要說再見了，都會祝福老朋友事業成功（success）、

獲得成就（accomplishment）、實現想望（fulfillment）。

字彙 應用搶先看：E-mail 會這麼寫！

1. I just wanted to inform you that I will soon be leaving ACE laboratories on June 9th to pursue my doctoral degree. It was an absolute pleasure working with all of you and I hope you all have a wonderful life and a successful career ahead of you.

   我要來跟您說我在六月九日就要離開艾思公司，要去攻讀我的博士學位了。能跟您們共事真的很開心，預祝您們接下來的生活精彩、事業成功！

2. It is with great sadness that I write this e-mail officially announcing that next Friday will be my last day working at ACE. It has been an honor and a pleasure working with you these past years. I wish every success in your future career!

   很難過地要來寫這封 e-mail 正式通知各位，下個星期五將是我在艾思公司工作的最後一天。能在過去這幾年來跟各位共事是我的榮幸，覺得很開心！在此預祝大家事業成功！

Part 8 合作／代理關係

字彙 應用開口說：電話要這麼講！ Track 143

M ▶ Manufacturer 廠商　D ▶ Distributor 代理商

M ▶ My old friend! I need to say goodbye to you! August 30th will be my last day working at ACE... .

廠商 ▶ 我的老朋友！我得要跟你說再見了！8 月 30 號將是我在艾思工作的最後一天……。

D ▶ No... I've worked with you for so many years! I never thought you'll be leaving!

代理商 ▶ 不……，我已經跟你一起工作那麼多年了，我從來沒想過你會離開啊！

M ▶ I know I'll leave here with a heavy heart but I think it's time for me to move forward to the next stage in my career! I want to thank you especially for your willingness to help me all the time in the past years!

廠商 ▶ 我知道離開了心情會很沉重，但我想該是時候朝我事業的下一個階段前進了！我要特別來謝謝你這些年一直都很願意幫助我！

D ▶ That's what I wanted to say!

代理商 ▶ 這句是我要說的耶！

M▶ Ha-ha...

D▶ Will there be any change in ACE's distributor policy?

M▶ Yeah, the new manager has suggested to reducing the number of distributors in Taiwan to help avoid territory overlap and competition between distributors. I agree with that and I believe you'll benefit from the new policy!

廠商▶ 哈哈……。

代理商▶ 那艾思的代理商策略會有改變嗎？

廠商▶ 有的，新經理建議縮減臺灣代理商的家數，這樣有助於避免代理商間區域重疊與競爭的問題。我也支持這麼做，而且我相信新政策對你們會有好處的！

Part 8 ｜合作／代理關係

字字 計較說分明

 Track 144

accomplishment [əˋkɑmplɪʃmənt]　*n.*　成就、完成、實現

例 We wish you all the very best of accomplishment in your career success!

祝您成就非凡、事業成功！

其他字義 才藝、技能

相關字 accomplish *[əˋkɑmplɪʃ]*　*v.*　完成、實現、使完美

---

appreciation [əˌpriʃɪˋeʃən]　*n.*　感謝

例 In appreciation of your time and effort, we are offering you the chance to win a tablet in a prize draw!

為了謝謝您所付出的時間與努力，我們將給您機會抽大獎、拿平板！

其他字義 欣賞、賞識、增值

相關字 appreciate *[əˋpriʃɪˌet]*　*v.*

---

fulfillment [fʊlˋfɪlmənt]　*n.*　完成、履行、實現、成就（感）

例 I wish you great success and fulfillment in your career!

祝您事業更加成功、更有成就！

相關字 fulfill *[fʊlˋfɪl]*　*v.*　執行、履行、實現、達到、滿足、使完整

honor [`ɑnɚ] *n.* 榮譽、光榮的事或人

例 It is a great honor for me to have this opportunity to speak at this conference.

能有機會在這場會議上發表演說，我深感榮幸。

其他字義 *v.* 承兌、允准、實踐

---

personnel [ˌpɝsn`ɛl] *n.* 人事、人員、員工

例 If you are not sure whom you should contact for certain inquiries, I am happy to be your primary contact and refer you to appropriate personnel.

如果您不確定哪些詢問要連絡誰，我很樂意當您的主要聯絡窗口，幫您轉給合適的人員。

---

pursue [pɚ`su] *v.* 追求、進行

例 I was extremely keen to pursue development of a professional career within the industry.

我以前很熱衷於在這產業裡追求專業生涯的發展。

ー職場英語ー

新多益雙篇閱讀均為英文商業書信，本書將
『考用』與『職場』強效連結，立即掌握書
寫『商用英文書信』的要訣！

書 系：Learn Smart 050
書 名：國貿與多益，一魚兩吃
定 價：NT$ 349元
ISBN：978-986-91915-3-1
規 格：平裝/336頁/17x23cm/雙色印刷

理論結合實務的專業手冊，便於如銀行行員、
外商會計、保險業...等相關工作者參考使用，
內容由淺入深，也適用於一般社會人士閱讀。

書 系：Leader 027
書 名：24天就能學會的基礎財金英文
定 價：NT$ 349元
ISBN：978-986-91914-6-3
規 格：平裝/336頁/17x23cm/雙色印刷

適合專業的餐飲從業人員自修英語，也適用於
餐飲相關科系教學；快速掌握餐飲業致勝關鍵
，從提升自我英語力開始！

書 系：Leader 030
書 名：一本搞定內外場餐飲英語（附MP3）
定 價：NT$ 380元
ISBN：978-986-91914-9-4
規 格：平裝/304頁/17x23cm/雙色印刷/附光碟

從入門到精通，完整掌握外貿全流程，以兩大篇
基礎入門篇、快速吸$篇，高效提升外貿業務職場
專業力＋英語力。

書 系：Leader 032
書 名：外貿業務英文（附MP3）
定 價：NT$ 380元
ISBN：978-986-92398-1-3
規 格：平裝/304頁/17x23cm/雙色印刷/附光碟

─職場英語─

一本專為航空地勤量身打造【職前準備+在職進修】的必備職場英語工具書！Upgrade工作英語能力 & 職場EQ！

書 系：Learn Smart 056
書 名：Ground Crew English航空地勤的每一天（MP3）
定 價：NT$ 380元
ISBN：978-986-91915-9-3
規 格：平裝/320頁/17x23cm/雙色印刷/附光碟

最基礎、最易學的餐飲口說英語！讓餐飲從業人員、餐飲科系師生、外商餐飲業的社會人士，都讚聲連連的英語工具書！

書 系：Leader 044
書 名：Easy & Basic餐飲口說英語(附MP3)
定 價：NT$ 380元
ISBN： 978-986-92856-3-6
規 格：平裝/304頁/17x23cm/雙色印刷/附光碟

最具指標性的空服員英語應試手冊，100%符合航空公司與個人特質的面試應答！擺脫一成不變的準備方式，加深考官印象，更替自己加分！

書 系：Learn Smart 059
書 名：王牌空服員100% 應試秘笈（附MP3）
定 價：NT$ 379元
ISBN：978-986-92855-2-0
規 格：平裝/288頁/17x23cm/雙色印刷/附光碟

最時尚、最「身歷其境感」的精華英語對答！秘書特助、行銷、公關，想要脫穎而出，不僅要加倍努力，還需要為你的職場英文實力加分！

書 系：Leader 049
書 名：時尚秘書英語（附MP3）
定 價：NT$ 380元
ISBN：978-986-92856-8-1
規 格：平裝/304頁/17x23cm/雙色印刷/附光碟

Learn Smart! 068

國貿人在全世界做生意的必備關鍵英單、句型 （附 MP3）

作　　者　劉美慧
發 行 人　周瑞德
執行總監　齊心瑀
企劃編輯　饒美君
校　　對　編輯部
封面構成　高鍾琪

內頁構成　菩薩蠻數位文化有限公司
印　　製　大亞彩色印刷製版股份有限公司
初　　版　2016 年 11 月
定　　價　新台幣 379 元
出　　版　倍斯特出版事業有限公司
電　　話　(02) 2351-2007
傳　　真　(02) 2351-0887
地　　址　100 台北市中正區福州街 1 號 10 樓之 2
E-mail　best.books.service@gmail.com
網　　址　www.bestbookstw.com

港澳地區總經銷　泛華發行代理有限公司
地　　址　香港新界將軍澳工業邨駿昌街 7 號 2 樓
電　　話　(852) 2798-2323
傳　　真　(852) 2796-5471

國家圖書館出版品預行編目資料

國貿人在全世界做生意的必備關鍵英
單、句型/ 劉美慧著. -- 初版. -- 臺北
市 : 倍斯特, 2016.11
　面 ; 　公分. -- (Learn smart!; 68)
ISBN 978-986-93766-1-7(平裝附光碟片)

1.商業英文 2.讀本

805.18　　　　　　　　105018631